DOCTOR WHO
THE FIVE DOCTORS

FANTASTIC
DOCTOR WHO
POSTER OFFER!

Pin up a magnificent full colour poster of Peter Davison as the Doctor, surrounded by a galaxy of Target novelisations – Free!

THIS OFFER EXCLUSIVE TO
DOCTOR WHO READERS

Just send £2.50 to cover postage and packing

> TO:
> Publicity Department
> W. H. Allen & Co. PLC
> 44 Hill Street
> London W1X 8LB

We will send you a **FREE FULL COLOUR POSTER**
on receipt of your order.
Please allow **28 days** for delivery.

Please send me a WORLD OF DOCTOR WHO poster.

I enclose £2.50 to cover postage and packing.

Name ——————————————————————————

Address ——————————————————————————

——————————————————————————

——————————————————————————

——————————————————————————

——————————————————————————

DOCTOR WHO
THE FIVE DOCTORS

Based on the BBC television programme by Terrance Dicks
by arrangement with the British Broadcasting Corporation

Terrance Dicks

No. 81
in the
Doctor Who Library

A TARGET BOOK

published by

the Paperback Division of
W. H. ALLEN & Co. PLC

A Target Book
Published in 1983
By the Paperback Division of
W. H. Allen & Co. PLC.
A Howard and Wyndham Company
44 Hill Street, London W1X 8LB
Third impression 1984

First published in Great Britain by
W. H. Allen & Co. Ltd 1983

Printed and bound in Great Britain by
Cox & Wyman Ltd, Reading

ISBN 0 426 19510 8

The producer of *The Five Doctors* was
John Nathan-Turner, the director was
Peter Moffatt.

Contents

1

The Game Begins

It was a place of ancient evil.

Somehow the evil seemed to hang in the air, like smoke or fog that long centuries had been unable to disperse. Along the length of one wall ran a massive control console with a monitor screen at its centre. The console's instrumentation was at once clumsy and complex. A scientist would have guessed it to be an early, primitive model of some highly sophisticated device. A huge Game Table dominated the centre of the room. It held a contoured model of a bleak and desolate landscape. In the centre, there was a Tower. Even in model form it looked sinister, threatening.

On a nearby table stood a carved, ivory box. Black-robed, black-gloved, the Player sat at the console operating controls untouched for many long years. The monitor screen lit up, filled only with the swirling mists of the temporal vortex. The black-robed Player worked with obsessive concentration, and at last his efforts met with some success. The swirling mists on the monitor screen resolved themselves into a blurred picture – a picture of a man. An old white-haired man in an old-fashioned frock-coat.

The Player leaned forward eagerly, tuning the controls, bringing the picture into clear focus.

It was time for the Game to begin.

The Doctor stepped back from the refurbished TARDIS console, surveying the results of his work with pride. Now in his fifth incarnation, he was a slender fair-haired young man, with a pleasant open face. As usual, he wore the costume of an Edwardian cricketer: striped trousers, fawn blazer with red piping, white cricketing sweater and an open-necked shirt. There was a fresh sprig of celery in his buttonhole.

One of the Doctor's two companions stood watching him suspiciously. Her name was Tegan Jovanka and she was an Australian air hostess. Tegan's experience of travelling with the Doctor had convinced her that (a) he didn't know what was going on most of the time, and (b) when he did get things right it was more by luck than judgement.

The Doctor had been repairing the TARDIS console which had suffered badly in a recent Cybermen attack. He had assured Tegan that the TARDIS was now even better than new, a claim Tegan viewed with her usual scepticism.

Feeling Tegan's eyes on the back of his neck, the Doctor turned. 'There we are then!'

'Finished?'

Proudly the Doctor patted the gleaming console. 'Yes. Looks rather splendid, doesn't it?'

Tegan had more practical concern. 'Will the TARDIS work properly now?'

'Of course,' said the Doctor airily. Catching

8

Tegan's eye he added. 'Once everything's run in, that is . . .'

'Did you repair the TARDIS or didn't you?'

'The TARDIS is more than just a machine, you know. It's like a person. It needs coaxing, persuading, encouraging.'

'In other words, the TARDIS is just as unreliable?'

'You have so little faith, Tegan.'

'Do you blame me?' asked Tegan bitterly. 'The amount of trouble you've landed me in, one way and another.'

Hurriedly the Doctor opened the main doors and slipped out of the TARDIS.

Once outside, the Doctor stood looking around him, surveying the peaceful scene with quiet enjoyment. The TARDIS stood amidst picturesque ivy-covered ruins. There was scarcely a breeze to stir the leaves and the tall grass. It might almost have been a fine summer afternoon on Earth, thought the Doctor. Except for the faint purple haze that hung in the air. Even this, exotic though it was, seemed somehow to add to the atmosphere of reassuring calm.

Turlough, the Doctor's other companion, sat with his back against a ruined wall, peacefully sketching. He was a thin-faced, sandy-haired young man, in the blazer and flannels of his public school, good-looking in a faintly untrustworthy way. For the moment, however, Turlough appeared to be in an exceptionally good mood. 'It really is marvellous here. I feel so calm and relaxed!'

'It's the high bombardment of positive ions in the atmosphere,' said the Doctor.

Tegan had followed the Doctor from the TARDIS

9

and she came over to join them, sniffing the air. 'It's like Earth, after a thunderstorm.'

'Same cause, same reason.'

Tegan looked round, her irritation fading in the peaceful atmosphere. 'It's beautiful here.'

The Doctor nodded. 'For some, the Eye of Orion is the most tranquil place in the Universe.'

Turlough yawned and stretched. 'Can't we stay here, Doctor?'

'Why not – for a while at least. We could all do with a rest.'

They stood for a moment in a companionable silence, drinking in the atmosphere of peace and tranquillity. It was the last peace of mind they were to enjoy for a very long time.

The Player made a final adjustment and the picture on the monitor sprang sharply into focus. It showed a white-haired frock-coated old man, bending over a rose-bush, secateurs in hand, face totally absorbed. It was an old face, lined and wrinkled, yet somehow alert and vital at the same time. The blue eyes were bright with intelligence. The commanding beak of the nose gave the old man a haughty, imperious air.

The Player smiled in cruel satisfaction.

The old man in the garden was known as the Doctor – a Doctor nearing the end of his first incarnation. The Doctor sensed that the end was near. He had come to this place to prepare himself, to say farewell to a body and a personality almost worn out by now, to prepare himself for the birth of a new self. Here in this peaceful garden he could prune his roses, and care for his bees.

10

He could enjoy a time of peace, of semi-retirement, before returning to the mainstream of his life and preparing to face the coming change.

Suddenly the old man tensed. Something was wrong. Something evil, some alien presence had come into his peaceful retreat. It seemed to be some kind of obelisk, rolling and tumbling towards him, growing larger and larger . . .

Suddenly it was almost upon him.

He turned to run but it was too late, far too late. 'No! No!' he shouted. The obelisk rolled forward, swallowing him up, absorbing him completely.

For a moment his distorted screaming face peered out from inside the obelisk. Then the obelisk rolled away, disappearing as rapidly as it had arrived.

The Player rose from the console, and went over to the Game Table. From the ivory box he took a tiny, beautifully carved figure. It represented a white-haired old man in an old-fashioned frock-coat. The Player put the little figure of Doctor One onto the board, pushing it towards the centre with a long rake.

The first piece was on the board.

In the Eye of Orion, the current Doctor, the fair-haired young man in the cricketer's blazer, gave a sudden involuntary cry, his face twisted in pain.

'Are you all right?' asked Turlough.

'Just a twinge of cosmic angst.'

Tegan stared at him. 'Cosmic how much?'

The Doctor looked puzzled. 'As if I'd – lost something . . .'

*

11

Brigadier Alastair Lethbridge-Stewart (Retired), one-time Commanding Officer of the United Nations Intelligence Taskforce, looked round the room that had once been his office. The annual UNIT Reunion was soon to take place. The Brigadier had mixed feelings about this sort of thing. Nice to see old friends of course, but odd to see them so changed.

Charlie Crichton came across the room towards the Brigadier, whisky bottle in hand. Strange to think he was now in command of UNIT. Bit stiff and formal old Charlie, thought the Brigadier, not realising how much he himself had mellowed over the years. Still, Charlie would learn – if he lived. In UNIT you encountered problems that weren't in anyone's rule book.

Crichton refilled the Brigadier's glass. 'Can't have our guest of honour running dry.'

Crichton raised his glass. 'To civilian life!'

'Hear, hear,' said the Brigadier. 'You know, I can't tell you how much I am looking forward to this reunion. The chance to meet old friends again.'

Brigadier Crichton put down his glass. 'There's one chap we've been trying to get hold of for ages. Mysterious sort of fellow. Used to be your Unpaid Scientific Adviser.'

The Brigadier smiled. 'Ah, the Doctor.'

'That's right. The Doctor!'

The Brigadier smiled reminiscently. 'Wonderful chap. All of them.'

Crichton looked curiously at him. 'Them? More than one, was there?'

'Well, yes and no,' said the Brigadier.

To his relief, they were interrupted by the buzz of the desk intercom.

Crichton flicked the switch. 'Yes?'

The voice of the duty-sergeant crackled out. 'Excuse me, sir, Sorry to interrupt. Someone's arrived.'

'I'm not expecting anyone. Who is it?'

There was a tinge of desperation in the sergeant's voice. 'I'm not sure, sir. He insists on seeing Brigadier Lethbridge-Stewart.' The tone of the sergeant's voice changed, as he addressed the unseen intruder. 'I'm sorry, sir, you're not allowed in there.'

'What?' said a familiar voice indignantly. 'Me? Not allowed? I'm allowed everywhere. Just get out of the way, will you? Thank you!'

The office door was flung open and a little figure popped inside eluding the grasp of the UNIT sergeant. The newcomer looked swiftly round the room. 'Brigadier!' He rushed across to them and shook hands warmly.

'Good heavens,' said the Brigadier faintly. 'Is it really you?'

'For once I've been able to steer the TARDIS correctly, and here I am!'

Brigadier Crichton caught the duty-sergeant's eye. 'It's all right, Sergeant.'

'Yessir,' said the sergeant woodenly and withdrew.

Crichton studied the newcomer curiously. He saw an odd-looking little fellow in a shabby old frock coat and rather baggy check trousers. Untidy black hair hung in a fringe over his forehead, and his dark brown eyes seemed humorous and sad at the same time.

The little man looked hopefully up at the Brigadier. 'I'm not too late, am I?'

'What for?'

'Your speech, as guest of honour.'

13

Brigadier Crichton looked at him in astonishment. 'How did you know the Brigadier would be here?'

'Saw it in *The Times*.'

'Impossible. The reporter's still here.'

'Tomorrow's *Times*,' said the little man witheringly. He turned to the Brigadier. 'Who is this fellow?'

'Colonel Crichton. My replacement.'

The little man sniffed. 'Mine was pretty unpromising too!'

Hastily, the Brigadier took the newcomer's arm. 'Come along, Doctor, we'll just take a stroll around the grounds.' He looked apologetically at Crichton. 'Excuse us for a moment. I'm awfully sorry about this.' He urged the newcomer to the door.

The little man stopped on the threshold and glanced around the office. 'You've had the place redecorated, haven't you. I don't like it!'

'Come on, Doctor,' said the Brigadier, and dragged him away.

As they went out, the UNIT sergeant came into the room. 'Everything all right, sir?'

'What the blazes is going on, Sergeant? Who was that strange little man?'

The sergeant answered. 'That was the Doctor.'

The Doctor and the Brigadier strolled through the formal grounds of UNIT HQ talking animatedly. To the Brigadier, this was the first, the original Doctor. The one he'd encountered in the London Underground during that terrible adventure with the Yeti. The one who had helped him defeat the invasion of the Cybermen. The Doctor who had reappeared one day, to defeat the menace of Omega in uneasy collabora-

14

tion with his other selves. They were discussing these adventures and more as they strolled round the stiffly formal grounds with their neatly raked gravel paths and flowers that seemed to be standing to attention.

'Yes indeed, Doctor,' the Brigadier was saying. 'Yeti, Cybermen. We've seen some times . . .'

'And Omega! Don't forget Omega!'

'As if I could.'

'And the terrible Zodin.'

'Who?'

'No, of course, you weren't concerned with her, were you? She happened in your future.' The Doctor came to a halt. 'I think it's time I said goodbye, Brigadier. I really shouldn't be here at all. I'm not exactly breaking the Laws of Time, but I'm bending them a little.'

'You never did bother very much about rules, Doctor, not as I remember.' The Brigadier noticed that the Doctor was staring fixedly at something over his shoulder. 'What's the matter?'

The Doctor pointed. 'Look!'

The Brigadier turned. A black obelisk was tumbling down the path towards them. 'What is it, Doctor?'

'I think our past is catching up with us, Brigadier. Or maybe it's our future. Come on, run!'

They began haring down the path. The obelisk tumbled after them at terrifying speed. The Doctor ran faster, the Brigadier panting along after him. 'Dammit, Doctor, I'm too old for this sort of thing.'

'Hurry Brigadier! We must get to the TARDIS before it's too late.'

The Doctor turned a corner, and found himself in a cul-de-sac. The path ended in a high wall. He turned, bumped into the Brigadier and the obelisk was upon them. It swallowed them up. For a moment their distorted faces could be seen inside it, then the obelisk tumbled rapidly into the distance, and disappeared.

The black-gloved hand of the Player took two more pieces from the box. A tiny figure in frock-coat and baggy trousers and a military-looking man with a neat moustache. The rake pushed the two pieces out onto the board. The Player returned to the console.

The Game was under way now.

But there was more, much more, to be done.

2

Pawns in the Game

'Over here, Tegan,' called Turlough. 'Quickly – the Doctor's ill!'

The Doctor was leaning against a ruined wall, his face twisted with pain.

Tegan ran up to him. 'Doctor, what is it?'

He stared at her – or rather, through her.

'Fading,' he whispered. 'All fading.'

'What's fading?'

'Great chunks of my past. Detaching themselves, like melting icebergs.'

Tegan turned almost angrily to Turlough. 'Don't just stand there. Do something to help him!'

'What am I supposed to do?'

Tegan saw from Turlough's face that he was as confused and frightened as she was herself.

Dimly aware of the wrangle, the Doctor managed a weak smile. 'Don't look so worried, you two. I'll have it all worked out soon. Everything's all right, you know. Everything is quite all right.' He fainted.

Elsewhere in space and time, on the planet Earth, the Doctor's third incarnation was driving very fast along a long straight road. This particular Doctor was a tall figure with a young-old face and a mane of prematurely white hair. He wore a velvet smoking-jacket and an open-necked shirt. The outfit was completed by a rather flamboyant checkered cloak. Doctor Three was something of a dandy.

The car he was driving was a vintage Edwardian roadster nicknamed 'Bessie'. It was moving at an impossible speed for so ancient a vehicle. This was because, over the years, the Doctor had tinkered with the engine to such an extent that he had virtually rebuilt it. Bessie now had a turn of speed that left racing cars standing. Indeed, at this very moment, the Doctor was driving Bessie on a privately owned stretch of road used to test racing engines. Just as well, since every possible speed limit had been well and truly shattered.

Suddenly, the Doctor spotted what looked like an obstruction in the road ahead. The obstruction, which appeared to be some kind of obelisk, was actually speeding down the road towards him.

'Great balls of fire!' said the Doctor. He threw the car into a spectacular skid-turn which made the tyres shriek protestingly.

Seconds later, the Doctor was streaking down the road in the opposite direction, leaving a black skid-mark on the road behind him, and a smell of burning rubber in the air. He checked his driving mirror and saw, with indignant surprise, that the obelisk was tumbling rapidly down the road in pursuit – and it was gaining fast.

'Right!' said the Doctor. He put Bessie into overdrive. The car shot off down the road, accelerating at an incredible rate. The Doctor looked in his mirror, noting with grim satisfaction that the obelisk was now dwindling back into the distance. It became smaller, smaller, and then disappeared.

He slowed the car, patting the dashboard. 'Good old Bessie.' He glanced over his shoulder, but the road behind him was reassuringly empty. 'I wonder what it was . . .' He returned his attention to the road ahead. And there was the obelisk – bearing down upon him.

He spun the wheel for another turn, but far too late this time.

Car and Doctor disappeared inside the obelisk.

The black-gloved hand put another piece on the board.

In the Eye of Orion Tegan and Turlough knelt worriedly by the Doctor. To their immense relief he opened his eyes and stared vacantly up at them.

'What's happening to him?' whispered Tegan. 'What are we going to do?'

'Search me. He doesn't seem to be ill exactly. It's more like some kind of psychic attack.'

'I am being diminished,' said the Doctor suddenly. 'Whittled away, piece by piece.' His voice was faint but calm, as if making some interesting scientific observation. 'A man is the sum of his memories, you know, and a Time Lord even more so.'

He struggled to sit up, and Tegan supported him. 'Doctor, what can we do to help you?'

'Get me into the TARDIS. . . I have to find. . . to find. . .'

Between them, Tegan and Turlough got the Doctor to his feet.

'Find what?' asked Turlough.

'My other selves. . .'

The Doctor slumped back in their arms.

Tegan looked at Turlough. 'What does he mean?'

Turlough shrugged.

Half dragging, half carrying, they helped the Doctor towards the TARDIS

The Player sat back. Three of the main pieces were now on the board – two more to go. But first he would allow himself a little diversion. He would pick up a pawn. Insignificant, valueless, fit only for sacrifice. It could be quite amusing . . .

The Player's hands glided over the controls. The swirling time-mists cleared, revealing the face of an attractive dark-haired girl.

Sarah Jane Smith, freelance journalist, opened the front door of her flat and looked out at the day. Not particularly bright, but at least it wasn't actually raining. She was on her way to see a magazine editor to discuss an important assignment. Her little car had chosen the previous evening to stage a total break-down. She'd have to travel by bus, which meant a walk and a wait at the bus stop. She didn't want to arrive at the meeting all soggy . . .

Sarah's rambling thoughts were interrupted by the appearance of a sort of squared-off metal dog with disc aerials for ears and a long thin antenna for a tail.

K9 was, in reality, a mobile self-powered computer with defensive capabilities. He was a souvenir of Sarah's former association with that traveller in time and space known as the Doctor.

Looking down Sarah saw that K9 was on full alert.

'What's the matter, K9?'

'Danger, Mistress.'

'What?'

'I sense danger, Mistress. Telepathic trace faint, but rapidly increasing in strength. Do not go out!'

Sarah knelt beside K9. 'What *kind* of danger?'

'Regret – more positive data not available.'

'I can't just stay at home all day,' said Sarah helplessly. 'Can't you give me some reason?'

'Negative, Mistress. Data analysis shows too many variables.' K9's voice became urgent. 'Danger readings now becoming much higher. Suggestion, Mistress: take me with you.'

'Honestly, I can't. The car's in dock and I'm going on the bus.'

Sarah turned to leave.

K9 glided forward. 'There *is* danger, Mistress,' he insisted. 'My sensors tell me it is now extreme. The Doctor is involved.'

Sarah frowned. Her parting with the Doctor had been abrupt, and as far as she was concerned, final. 'Now I know you're imagining things, K9. I'll see you later.'

Stepping quickly past K9 she closed the door.

K9's voice came faintly from behind the door. 'Doctor . . . danger . . . Doctor . . . Mistress . . .'

Hardening her heart, Sarah ignored it, and set off for the bus stop.

Doctor, indeed, she thought as she walked down the quiet suburban road. After years of companionship and innumerable shared dangers, the Doctor had suddenly rushed off to Gallifrey in response to some mysterious summons, leaving Sarah behind. She had been insisting for some time that all she wanted was to return to Earth and lead a quiet life, but the abruptness of the parting had left Sarah feeling abandoned, and more than a little resentful.

And he needn't think he can get round me by sending me a crated-up K9 either, thought Sarah as she peered down the road in search of her bus. She seemed to be in luck, for there was something moving ahead. It came nearer and nearer.

Too late, Sarah saw that it wasn't a bus at all, but a strange, tumbling black obelisk. She screamed, and turned to run, but it was much too late . . .

The woman called Susan Campbell, who had once been known as Susan Foreman, walked through the streets of New London on the way to market. Looking about her she marvelled at how swiftly the city had recovered from the devastation of the Dalek attack.

Gleaming new buildings were everywhere, the old bombed sites had all been cleared. Those which hadn't been used as sites for new buildings had been turned into parks and gardens. It was a smaller London – it would be many years before population rose anywhere near its old levels – but it was a greener, far more attractive one.

Life had been hard at first. For many years she had seen very little of her husband David, who was a prominent figure in the Reconstruction Government. But gradually life had returned to normal. Now Susan and David and their three children could look forward to a more peaceful life. These days it seldom occurred to Susan that this wasn't really her world at all, that she had originally come here almost by chance in the company of the old man she sometimes called Grand-father, and everyone else called the Doctor.

It was still early, and the street was deserted.

Susan stopped dead, staring ahead of her.

Something very odd had appeared at the far end of the street.

A strange alien shape, tumbling over and over, was rushing straight towards her.

Susan felt the kind of terror she had not felt for many years. Somehow the unknown had come to claim her, shattering her normal life once again. As the obelisk swallowed her up, her last despairing thoughts were of the Doctor.

The Player stepped back from the Game Table, smiling coldly. Two more pawns in place.

The three main pieces were already on the board.

He had only to add the fourth and the fifth would follow, drawn by the attraction of his other selves, by the need to be whole.

He must find and transfer the fourth piece . . .

He returned to the console and leaned forward, his face tense with concentration. The swirling time-mists on the monitor cleared at last, to show a river and a boat.

The tall curly-haired man with the wide staring eyes propelled the punt along the backwaters of the river Cam with steady thrusts of the long pole. He wore com-fortable Bohemian-looking clothes, a loose coat with an open-necked shirt. A broad-brimmed soft hat was jammed on the back of his head, and an incredibly long scarf looped about his neck. This was the Doctor in his fourth incarnation. As might have been expected, he had something of all his previous selves about him: the intellectual arrogance of the first, the humour of the second, and something of the elegance of the third, though in a more relaxed and informal style.

Lolling back on cushions in the front of the boat, a girl was watching the Doctor's efforts with amused admiration. She was on the small side, aristocratically beautiful, with long fair hair above a high forehead. This was Romana, the Doctor's Time Lady companion.

They were gliding along the part of the river known as the Backs, so called because the river ran between the backs of the various Cambridge colleges. On either side, green lawns sloped up to elegant old buildings.

The Doctor made an expansive gesture, almost overbalancing in the process. 'Wordsworth!' he said dramatically. 'Rutherford, Christopher Smart, Andrew Marvell, Judge Jeffries, Owen Chadwick . . .'

Romana trailed a hand in the cool water. 'Who?'

'Owen Chadwick. Economist, I think. They were all here, you know, some of the finest minds, the greatest intellectual labourers in the history of Earth.'

Romana nodded. 'Isaac Newton, of course.'

'Oh yes, definitely Newton.'

The Doctor thrust the pole into the river bed, and the punt shot forward.

'For every action there must be an equal and opposite re-action,' quoted Romana solemnly.

'Quite right!'

'So Newton invented punting?'

'Oh yes, there was no limit to old Isaac's genius.'

The punt glided smoothly forwards and Romana said, 'Isn't it wonderful how something so primitive can be so . . .'

'Civilised?'

'No, simple. You just push in one direction and the boat moves in the other.' She looked about her. 'I do love the Earth in spring. The leaves, the colours . . .'

'It's almost October,' said the Doctor apologetically.

'I thought you said we were coming here for May week?'

'I did – though mind you, May week's in June.'

'I'm confused.'

'So was the TARDIS.'

Romana tried again. 'I do love the autumn,' she said poetically. 'The leaves, the colours . . .'

'Well, never mind! If only the TARDIS was as simple as a punt! No co-ordinates, no dimensional stabilisers. Just the water, the punt, a strong pair of hands and a pole. Nothing can possibly go wrong.'

Romana was peering ahead. 'What's that under the bridge, Doctor. Another boat?'

The Doctor leaned forward to look, at the same time thrusting the pole hard into the river bed. It stuck fast in a soft patch. Distracted by the sight of a black obelisk rolling across the water towards him, the Doctor let go of the pole. The boat drifted helplessly on and the obelisk swallowed up both its occupants.

Slowly the empty punt drifted beneath the bridge.

Lights flashed on the console. A warning siren hooted, shattering the silence. The Player worked frantically at the controls. Something had gone wrong – badly wrong. Unless he could stabilise the situation there was grave danger of temporal instability. He worked feverishly, and at last the siren was stilled and the warning lights ceased to flash. The Player leaned back, exhausted.

On the monitor screen he could see the distorted, slowly rotating shapes of the Doctor and Romana. They were trapped in a freak eddy in the vortex – and he had neither the skill nor the energy to free them. But although it was a set-back, it was by no means complete disaster. There were already three Doctors on the board. And there were the companions, those luckless pawns in the game. Enemies, old and new, were already in place. One more piece on the board, and the game could enter the next, most vital phase.

The Player leaned forwards and worked on the controls. The trapped fourth Doctor faded and the fifth appeared . . .

3

Death Zone

Once inside the TARDIS, the Doctor pulled free from Tegan and Turlough, and staggered over to the centre console. Eyes staring blankly ahead, he punched up co-ordinates and set the TARDIS in motion. It seemed almost as if he was operating the TARDIS in his sleep. As the time rotor began its rise and fall, the Doctor slid gently to the ground.

'Oh no!' gasped Tegan.

Turlough knelt beside the Doctor, taking his pulse. It was strong and steady. For confirmation, Turlough put a hand on the Doctor's chest and felt a steady thump-thump. He moved his hand to the other side, and felt another heartbeat, equally strong. He looked up in astonishment at Tegan who said briefly, 'Two hearts!'

Turlough straightened up. 'I see. Well, his body seems to be all right, as far as I can tell . . . He seems to be just . . . fading away.' He looked angrily at Tegan. 'Why did he have to set the TARDIS moving? We were safe before he did that.'

Tegan wasn't listening. She was staring in horror at the Doctor's unconscious body. The Doctor really was fading away – quite literally.

His body was actually becoming transparent, as he faded slowly out of existence.

Tegan knelt and grasped the already insubstantial hand. *'Doctor!'*

The Doctor responded, and she felt his hand become solid and real inside her own.

She looked in anguish up at Turlough. 'What's going on?'

Turlough pointed to the time rotor. It had stopped moving. 'We've landed.'

He switched on the scanner. They saw a stretch of bleak and threatening landscape. At its centre, not far away, there loomed a dark and sinister tower.

The Player gave a great sigh of relief. As he had hoped, the presence of three of the Doctor's selves had been powerful enough to draw him to their side, even though the fourth Doctor was still missing. Drawn irresistibly by his need to be whole again, the Doctor had delivered himself and his companions into the trap.

The Player took a model Doctor, and a model Tegan and Turlough from the box and pushed them on to the Game Table.

While Tegan kept a watchful eye on the Doctor, Turlough carried out a quick check on the TARDIS control console.

'As far as I can make out from the instruments, we're nowhere and no-time.'

'The Doctor probably forgot to reconnect something,' said Tegan gloomily.

Turlough shook his head. 'The instruments appear

28

to be working perfectly. They just won't tell us anything. The TARDIS is paralysed.'

'So how did we get here? And what do we do now?'

Turlough looked sombrely down at the Doctor. He was still unconscious, and breathing heavily, but at least he was *there*.

'I suppose we just wait, till the Doctor recovers.'

'And if he doesn't?' asked Tegan.

Turlough had no answer.

Magnificent in full presidential regalia, President Borusa strode through the corridors of the Capitol, acknowledging the respectful greetings of passing Time Lords with the briefest of nods. The expression on the long intellectual face was positively thunderous. Lord President Borusa was in a very bad mood indeed.

He reached the presidential conference room, swept past the guards at the door and paused on the threshold. The conference room was small, but furnished with the greatest luxury. There was a transmat booth, discreetly tucked away in one corner. A highly polished oval conference table occupied the centre of the room with high-backed chairs ranged around it. The only ornaments were an antique harp on a stand, and an ancient painting on the wall. Two of the chairs were already occupied, one by Chancellor Flavia, the other by the Castellan.

Borusa surveyed them coldly, then took his place in the throne-like presidential chair at the head of the conference table. 'Well?'

The Castellan said respectfully, 'He has arrived, Lord President.'

The news gave Borusa no pleasure. 'Involving this – person does not please me.'

The Castellan's voice was still respectful, but it held an underlying firmness. 'The Constitution clearly states that when, in Emergency Session, the Members of the Inner Council are unanimous – '

'As indeed we are,' interrupted Chancellor Flavia crisply. She was a small neat woman, with an immensely strong will.

Borusa waved them both to silence. 'Yes, yes, in such an event, the President can be overruled. I know that ridiculous clause.' Borusa sighed with exaggerated weariness. 'Very well, have him enter.'

The Castellan touched the mini-control console built into the arm of his chair. Everyone looked expectantly at the door.

Seconds later it opened. A figure stood in the doorway. A tall figure, elegant in black velvet, his arrogantly handsome features set off by a neatly pointed black beard.

The Master.

He stood looking at the three Time Lords for a moment, then gave an exaggeratedly courtly bow. 'Lord President, Castellan, Chancellor Flavia. This is a very great, may I say, a most unexpected honour.'

The deep musical voice had an insolently amused undertone like the purr of a great black cat. It was with catlike litheness that the Master strolled across the room. 'I may be seated?' Without waiting for either permission or reply, the Master dropped gracefully into the vacant chair and looked insolently around the little group. 'Now what can I do for you?'

Borusa leaned forward, fixing the Master with the

piercing look that had reduced many a Time Lord opponent to terrified silence. 'You are one of the most evil and corrupt beings our Time Lord race has ever produced. Your crimes are without number, your villainy without end.'

The Master nodded graciously, like someone receiving a well deserved compliment.

Restraining himself with a visible effort, Borusa continued, 'Nevertheless, we are prepared to offer you a full and free pardon.'

If Borusa expected surprise or gratitude, he was to be disappointed. The Master raised an eyebrow. 'What makes you think I want your forgiveness?'

'We can offer you an alternative to your renegade existence,' said the Castellan bluntly.

'Indeed?' The Master raised an eyebrow. Beneath the assumed calm his mind was racing furiously. The Time Lords needed him, that was obvious. And if that was the case, they must know that no ordinary reward would persuade him to serve them. Could it be . . .

Borusa spoke, completing the Master's thought. 'Regeneration. A whole new life cycle.'

It was all that the Master could do not to show his excitement. Regeneration! In the course of a spectacularly criminal existence, the Master had used up all his allotted regenerations with record speed. He had only survived in his present form by ruthlessly hijacking the body of another. Unfortunately it was not a Time Lord body. When it began to age and decay, as it inevitably would, the Master would be forced to steal another body, and then another. It was a ghoulish sort of existence at best, and the Master wanted desperately to be free of it. With a fierce effort

31

of will, he forced himself to remain calm. 'I see . . .
And what must I do?'

Borusa blurted out the incredible truth. 'Rescue the
Doctor.'

The first Doctor was wandering in a nightmare. Old,
white-haired and frail, yet somehow indomitable, he
staggered on through endless metal corridors. The
silver, polished walls seemed to be set at odd, discon-
certing angles, presenting a mind-bending sense of
unreality. All around him he saw distorted versions of
his own reflection. He plodded on. There was an
answer somewhere, a reason behind this mystery, and
eventually he would find it. He had never given up
yet, and he was too old to change.

Suddenly he paused, peering ahead.

Someone was moving towards him.

The Doctor stepped back, flattening himself against
an angle of wall. A towering distorted shape moved
along the corridors. The shape came nearer, the
twisted reflections danced – and suddenly a slender
dark-haired young woman appeared from round the
corner.

The Doctor looked at her in astonishment for a
moment, and then stepped forward, 'Susan? Surely
it's Susan?'

The young woman threw herself into his arms with
a force that almost knocked him over. 'Grandfather!
Thank goodness I've found you! How did we get here?
What's happening?'

Gently the Doctor disengaged himself. 'I wish I
knew, my dear.'

'As soon as I found myself in this horrible place I

started looking for you. Somehow I knew you were here.'

'Yes, yes,' said the Doctor, with a touch of his old tetchiness. 'The important question now is, where are we and why?'

Susan looked despairingly around. There was a patch of light at the corridor junction behind them, and suddenly a shadow fell across it.

The shadow of a Dalek.

Susan pointed. 'Look! We must be on Skaro!'

The Doctor, as usual, refused to take anything for granted. 'We were brought here. Perhaps the Dalek was brought here too.'

Before Susan could answer the Dalek glided round the corner. She gave a gasp of horror at the sight of the squat metal-studded pepper-pot shape, with the jutting sucker arm and gun stick. The constantly swivelling eye-stalk registered their presence immediately.

The harsh grating Dalek voice echoed through the metal corridors. 'Halt! Halt at once or you will be exterminated!'

'Run, Doctor!' shouted Susan.

Separating to present smaller targets, ducking and weaving and zigzagging, the Doctor and Susan fled. As they ran, their distorted reflections moved with them.

Confused by the constantly changing images, the Dalek fired again and again, the blasts echoing along the metal corridors. Unfortunately, it had registered Susan's use of the Doctor's name. As it pursued them along the corridors, the metallic voice grated, 'It is the Doctor! The Doctor must be destroyed! Exterminate! Exterminate! Exterminate!'

*

A monitor screen lit up on one wall of the conference room. It showed the Mountains of Gallifrey. At the inaccessible centre was a patch of sinister blackness.

'The Death Zone,' said Borusa simply.

The Master stroked his beard. 'Ah yes. The black secret at the centre of your Time Lord paradise.'

'Recently,' said the Castellan, 'the Death Zone has become – reactivated. Somehow it is draining energy from the Eye of Harmony.'

'To such an extent,' said Chancellor Flavia, 'that all Gallifrey is endangered.'

The Eye of Harmony was the precious Time Lord energy source, formed from the nucleus of a Black Hole, stabilised by Rassilon untold years ago.

Borusa stared broodingly at the map of the Zone. 'We must know what is happening there.'

'Did it occur to you to go and look?'

'Two of the High Council entered the Zone to investigate. Neither one returned.'

'So you sent for the Doctor.' The Master knew that for many years the Time Lords had used the Doctor, often against his will, as a kind of cosmic trouble-shooter.

'We *looked* for the Doctor,' corrected the Castellan. 'But we discovered that the Doctor no longer existed, in any of his regenerations,' Borusa said flatly. 'It appears that the Doctor has been taken out of space and time.'

The Castellan touched a control in his chair. The map of the Death Zone was replaced by a distorted, swirling vision of the fourth Doctor, whose punting trip had been so suddenly interrupted. 'We believe that the attempt to lift *this* regeneration from his time-stream was unsuccessful. He is trapped in a time-eddy, and there he must stay until we find and free his other selves.'

'And if you cannot?' There was no reply, and the Master laughed softly. 'A cosmos without the Doctor. It scarcely bears thinking about!' He considered for a moment. 'You can get me into the Zone?'

The Castellan nodded to the transmat booth in the corner. 'We have a power-boosted open-ended transmat beam.'

'What makes you believe the Doctor's other selves are in the Zone?'

Borusa shrugged. 'Their time-traces converge there.'

The Master nodded thoughtfully. 'Why me?'

'We needed someone cunning, ruthless, experienced, determined. . .'

'And disposable?' suggested the Master.

'Not at all,' said the Castellan blandly. 'You would be useless to us dead.'

Chancellor Flavia was becoming impatient. 'Will you go?'

For a long moment the Master made no reply.

Borusa leaned forward. *'Will you?'*

'And rescue the Doctor. . .' The Master smiled.

4

Unexpected Meeting

The Doctor was fading again. For some time now he had been pulsing in and out of existence, sometimes completely real and solid, at others insubstantial as a ghost. Tegan and Turlough knelt beside him, doing their best to will him back into being. It appeared that the Doctor could arrest the process by some kind of mental effort. The problem was to keep him conscious, and to persuade him to exert his will. In the Doctor's weakened condition, it wasn't easy.

'Come on, Doctor,' urged Tegan.

'Hold on,' shouted Turlough. 'Hold on!'

As if responding to the urgency in their voices, the Doctor opened his eyes, suddenly becoming real and solid again.

'Doctor, what's happening to you?' asked Tegan desperately.

The Doctor's voice was faint. 'Being sucked into the time vortex . . . Part of me there already . . . pulling the rest.'

He began to fade again.

'No!' shouted Tegan.

Suddenly the Doctor became solid again.

He started struggling to his feet. 'I mustn't sleep. Don't let me sleep . . .'

Susan and the first Doctor were still running through endless metal corridors, the angry Dalek at their heels. Its metallic voice echoed close behind them, shrieking orders, threats and warnings. 'Halt at once! You will be exterminated. Obey the Daleks!' And always the old, chilling battle-cry. 'Exterminate! Exterminate! Exterminate!'

They had been running for what seemed a very long time now, and the old man was almost exhausted. For the later stages of their flight, Susan had been helping, almost dragging him along. Sometimes the Dalek was close enough to fire at them, at others they managed to shake it off for a while. But Susan was all too aware that in the long run it was steadily gaining on them. The end was only a matter of time.

They turned a corner, only to find themselves in a kind of cul-de-sac, a metal wall barring the way ahead.

'It's a blind alley,' gasped Susan. 'Turn back, quickly.'

The old man's body might be exhausted, but his mind was as alert and active as ever. 'That may be precisely what we need.'

Susan tugged at his sleeve. 'Grandfather, let's get out of here. Please!'

The Doctor refused to move. 'Don't argue, there isn't time,' he said imperiously. 'Now, listen carefully, Susan. When I shout "Now!" help me to shove the Dalek down that alley. And when I shout "Drop!" – then *drop*. Understood?'

Susan opened her mouth to argue, caught the old man's eye and said meekly, 'Understood.'

The Doctor flattened himself against the wall, drawing Susan beside him.

The monotonous ranting of the Dalek was very close now. 'Halt! You will be exterminated!'

Suddenly it glided around the corner, very fast, moving a little way past them.

'Now!' shouted the Doctor.

They sprang out of hiding, ran up behind the Dalek and shoved it down the little blind alley with all their combined strength. The Dalek shot forward, eye-stalk swivelling to find its attackers, trying desperately to turn and bring its blaster to bear. 'Under attack. Under attack!' it screeched. Catching a distorted glimpse of the Doctor and Susan it began firing wildly.

'Drop!' shouted the Doctor.

They dropped, flattening themselves on to the floor, while energy-bolts roared and ricocheted over their heads. Then the inevitable happened. One of the energy-bolts ricocheting about the tiny blind alley bounced back and scored a direct hit on the Dalek itself, and it exploded in smoke and flame, blasting a substantial hole in the metal wall. They kept their heads down, waiting for the rain of fiery debris to subside. Finally the Doctor rose a little creakily to his feet, and helped Susan to stand up. The Dalek was no more than a pile of smoking metallic fragments.

The Doctor surveyed the remains with some satisfaction. 'It's very dangerous to fire energy weapons in an enclosed space,' he observed mildly. Not that it would have been any good warning the Dalek, he thought, even if he'd wanted to. Daleks never listen.

Susan was staring through the jagged hole in the wall. 'Look!'

The hole revealed a bleak and barren landscape, scarred and pitted like some ancient battlefield. In the distance there were jagged mountains, and in the middle of them, a dark and sinister tower. Both Susan and the Doctor recognised the Tower and landscape immediately, and looked at each other in horror. If there was a place worse than Skaro to find yourself in, this was it.

'The Dark Tower,' whispered the old man.

'We're on Gallifrey,' said Susan unbelievingly.

'In the Death Zone.'

'But why? Why were we brought here?'

The Doctor rallied, straightening up, and tugging at his lapels. 'Instinct, my dear, tells me that the answer to that question lies in the Tower. Come!'

Indomitable as ever, the old man led the way forward.

The Brigadier looked down at his little companion with an air of bitter reproach. 'Charming spot, Doctor!'

After their sudden abduction from the grounds of UNIT HQ, the second Doctor and the Brigadier had found themselves, apparently unharmed, in what looked like the ruins of some once-great city. A city that had been flattened, devastated by some long-past catastrophe, leaving behind only patches of rubble and the occasional broken wall. The whole area was dark and overcast. Occasionally there was a rumble of distant thunder, and jagged lightning bolts streaked across the sky. Thick patches of drifting fog added a sinister touch to the terrifying landscape.

Pushing back his fringe of untidy black hair, the little Doctor peered cautiously around him. 'My dear Brigadier, it's no use blaming me!'

'You attract trouble, Doctor,' said the Brigadier grimly. 'You always did! Where the devil are we?'

'I'm not sure yet,' said the Doctor mysteriously. 'But I have some very nasty suspicions.' Suddenly he pointed. 'What's that? Over there!'

The Brigadier shaded his eyes with his hands. He caught a fleeting glimpse of huge shapes, moving stealthily through the fog. The instincts of long-ago battlefields made him pull the Doctor into the shelter of a nearby wall. 'Something moving up ahead.'

'Keep down,' hissed the Doctor, and immediately popped his own head up for a better look.

They both crouched low, careful to keep close to the remains of the delapidated wall. So intent were they both on the threat out there in the distance that neither noticed when an enormous hand appeared through a hole in the wall and groped stealthily towards them.

It moved closer . . . closer . . . Suddenly it seized the Brigadier by the arm in a grip like that of a steel clamp. The Brigadier gave a yell of alarm. He leaped to his feet, and began desperately trying to pull himself free. The Doctor jumped up, and grabbed the Brigadier's other arm, pulling hard. But the unseen owner of the hand and arm was incredibly strong. Both Doctor and Brigadier were dragged remorselessly towards the hole.

Letting go of the Brigadier's arm, the Doctor looked round for a weapon. To his delight he spotted a chunk of metal piping half buried in the mud. Wrenching it free, he used it as a club, smashing again and again at the wrist of the unseen attacker. The great hand was jarred open, and the Brigadier was free. The Doctor tossed the length of piping aside and yelled, 'Run, Brigadier!'

They ran, stumbling across the rough ground, away from the threat behind the wall and the menacing shapes that lurked in the mist.

In the TARDIS, the fifth Doctor staggered towards the console. 'Signal,' he muttered. 'Must send signal . . .' He reeled, and Turlough caught him just in time. 'Doctor wake up! We need you to get us out of here.'

Gently Tegan shook the Doctor's shoulder. 'What signal, Doctor?'

The Doctor opened his eyes and stared blankly at her. 'Must send signal . . . find them. Must be . . . *whole.*' He stared at her in anguish. 'Help me!'

The tall man with the shock of white hair drove cautiously through the drifting mists. It was considerate of his unknown kidnapper to hijack Bessie as well, he thought. Thanks to the Doctor's many modifications, the little roadster was making good progress, even over this rough ground. Suddenly the fog thickened. The Doctor stopped the car for a moment. 'Now what?' He peered ahead, pulling his cloak collar up around his ears.

It was a bleak and barren landscape, churned and broken, and the road was little more than a rough track. There were mountains ahead, and the looming shape of some kind of tower. Grim suspicions were beginning to form in the Doctor's mind. He narrowed his eyes. Had he seen something moving in the dense patch of fog ahead?

Sarah Jane Smith stumbled miserably through the fog, picking her way through rough ground, broken up only by the occasional stunted tree. Black clouds rolled overhead, and lightning bolts seared across the sky. It was, thought Sarah, as unattractive a piece of landscape as she had ever seen. 'Oh, K9, why didn't I listen to you?' she moaned.

The fog pressed in on her threateningly. Somehow Sarah was convinced that there was something waiting in ambush, out there in the fog. She tripped over a chunk of broken branch and snatched it up, thinking it might serve as a weapon. Clutching her club, she took a cautious step forwards – and suddenly the ground vanished from beneath her feet. She had stepped clean over the edge of a ravine.

Sarah screamed, dropping the stick, and flailed out desperately in an attempt to regain her balance, but it was too late. She hurtled over the edge, scrabbling desperately for some kind of handhold. She managed to arrest her fall by clutching at a shrub growing from the cliff edge. But it was too slight to bear her weight. She felt it beginning to pull away. Sarah looked below. The ravine appeared to be bottomless, a deep fissure in the earth. If she fell she would probably be killed. Even if she survived, she would never get out again. The roots began to tear . . .

Then as if from nowhere a voice called, 'Hang on a minute. Catch hold of this!', and something dropped past her face. It was a rope!

Sarah grabbed it, saving herself just as the roots pulled free.

She looked up and saw a tall, white-haired figure looking down at her from the cliff edge. 'Hang on!'

Sarah heard the growl of an engine. Then came a steady pull on the rope, miraculously drawing her upwards.

She scrambled over the cliff-edge, and fell into the arms of the Doctor. 'I've never been so pleased to see anyone!'

'Me too,' said the familiar voice. 'But I really think we should move away from the edge!'

He drew her back towards safety. Sarah saw that the Doctor had tied the rope to Bessie and used the car to pull her up. He unfastened the rope and began coiling it neatly.

Sarah stared unbelievingly at him. 'Wait a minute – it's you!'

'Of course it's me. Hello, Sarah Jane.'

'No, but it's the *you* you!'

'That's right!'

This was undoubtedly the Doctor as Sarah had known him first, before that ghastly business with the spiders had triggered his regeneration.

'But you changed!'

The Doctor smiled. 'Did I?'

'Don't you remember? You became – all teeth and curls.'

The Doctor shuddered, visibly appalled by the prospect. 'Teeth and curls? Well, maybe I did – but I haven't yet.'

Suddenly Sarah could feel herself becoming very angry. 'I see. No, I don't – but never mind. Well, thanks very much for rescuing me, Doctor. Now maybe you'll explain just why I'm here to need rescuing?'

The Doctor smiled, thinking that Sarah hadn't changed. She had never been ready to accept the traditional role of the maiden in distress. 'Steady on, Sarah Jane. I'm not exactly here by choice myself.'

She gaped at him. 'You're not? Then what are we both doing here?'

'I'm not sure, yet,' said the Doctor darkly, 'though I have my suspicions.' He tossed the coiled rope into the back of the car. 'Come along, Sarah Jane, get in the car. I'll try to explain on the way.'

Supported by Tegan and Turlough, the fifth Doctor stared at the TARDIS console as if he had never seen it before in all his lives. 'I've got to . . . got to . . .' He looked almost indignantly at Tegan and Turlough – as if it was all their fault. 'What is it I've got to do?'

Tegan said, 'You were going on about some kind of signal.'

'And about being whole,' added Turlough.

'The signal. Yes, of course!'

'What's the signal *for*, Doctor?' asked Tegan. 'Who is it to?

'Recall signal,' said the Doctor with almost pathetic eagerness. 'They'll hear it. Yes, that'll bring them . . .'

He staggered again, clutching at the console for support and staring vaguely at the maze of controls. It was all too obvious that the Doctor didn't have the slightest idea what to do next.

Tegan spoke urgently. 'Listen, Doctor, tell us where the signal control is, so we can send it for you.'

The Doctor stared wildly at her. 'It's . . . it's . . .'

His hands groped blindly over the console for a moment, then he crashed to the floor.

5

Two Doctors

As she helped the tired old man across the rough ground, Susan was beginning to wonder if their situation had really improved very much. They had exchanged endless metal corridors for endless barren countryside. At the moment they were making their way through a desolate area strewn with boulders. Still, at least they'd got rid of the Dalek – though it was very possible that more Daleks waited in ambush somewhere ahead. The Doctor came to a sudden halt. He leaned gasping against a boulder.

'It's no good, Susan,' he said angrily, hating to admit his weakness. 'I shall have to rest.'

'Yes, of course, Grandfather, you stay there. I'll just go and see what things look like past these boulders.'

Susan walked a little way forwards to where the clump of boulders ended. The land sloped downwards a little. To her delight, there in a little hollow she saw a familiar square blue shape. She turned and called, 'Grandfather, look. Come and see!'

Wearily the Doctor heaved himself upright and came to join her. 'What is it?' He stared. 'Goodness me! The TARDIS!'

'What's the TARDIS doing here?'

The discovery had revived the old man's flagging energies. 'I suggest we go and find out,' he said sharply, and set off down the path.

The Doctor moaned and stirred and opened his eyes. 'He's conscious,' said Turlough gloomily. 'But only just.'

Tegan nodded. 'If only he'd recovered long enough to send that signal.'

Then to her utter astonishment, the outer door of the TARDIS opened. In marched a white-haired old man, key in hand. A slim dark-haired woman was close behind him.

Tegan and Turlough stared.

The newcomers stared back at them with an astonishment equal to their own.

Tegan jumped to her feet. 'Who are you?'

The old man snapped, 'More to the point, young woman, who are you?' He surveyed the little group with obvious disapproval. 'What are all you young people doing inside my TARDIS?'

Tegan pointed to the slight fair-haired figure stretched out on the floor. 'It's *his* TARDIS.'

'And who might he be?' asked the old man disdainfully.

Turlough got to his feet. 'He happens to be the Doctor.'

The old man gave a gasp of sheer astonishment. '*He's* the Doctor? Good grief!'

A little stiffly, he went down on one knee beside the unconscious Doctor, looking curiously into his face. The Doctor opened his eyes, and saw the lined old face looking down at him. 'You're here!' he said delightedly. 'You're here!' Reaching out to clasp the old man's

47

outstretched hands, he struggled into a sitting position.

'Evidently, evidently,' said the old man gruffly. 'Now, take it steadily, my boy. Let me help you up.'

It was as though the younger man was actually drawing strength from the elder, thought Tegan. You could almost see the life flooding back into the Doctor's body.

The Doctor hung onto the old man's hand for a moment, steadying himself. 'I was trying to send you the recall signal . . .'

'Never mind about that. How do you come to be here?'

The Doctor looked puzzled. 'I'm not sure . . . the TARDIS . . . I was drawn here, I think. I don't really know.'

'Well, it doesn't matter. The point is, we're here.'

Susan put a hand on the old man's arm. She was looking in astonishment at the Doctor's youthful face. 'Is he really . . .'

The old man said wryly, 'Me? Yes, I'm afraid so.' He turned to the Doctor. 'Regeneration?'

'Fourth.'

'Goodness me. So, there are five of us now! By the way, this is Susan.'

'Yes,' said the Doctor gently. 'I know.' He smiled affectionately at Susan, a face from a past so far away it seemed hardly real.

The old man looked at the Doctor's two companions. 'And you are?'

'Turlough,' said Turlough briefly, not sure what was going on.

Tegan said, 'And I'm Tegan Jovanka. And who might you be?'

'I might be any number of things, young lady. As it happens, I am the Doctor. The original, you might say. Number One!'

He drew himself up proudly, hands tugging at his lapels.

It wasn't so much the first Doctor's existence that puzzled Tegan. By now she was familiar with the concept of regeneration. It was his presence, here and now. 'But you shouldn't be here, with him, at the same time – should you?'

Vigorously the old man shook his head. 'Certainly not!'

The Doctor said, 'It only happens in the gravest of emergencies – '

'Like now,' completed Doctor One. 'Now, just make yourself useful, will you, young woman. This young fellow looks as if he needs some refreshment, and I know Susan and I do.'

Tegan glared at him in sheer disbelief. 'Now just you hang on a minute,' she began dangerously.

Hurriedly the Doctor intervened. 'Tegan, *please*. He gets a bit – tetchy, sometimes. Turlough will help – won't you, Turlough?'

Exchanging mutinous glances, Tegan and Turlough left by the inner door.

The old man put his hand on the Doctor's shoulder. 'Now then, young fellow, tell me all about it.'

There was an elaborate golden badge in Chancellor Flavia's hand. She held it out to the Master. 'The Seal of the High Council. It will help convince the Doctors of your good faith.'

It would take a lot more than a seal, however

49

eminent, to do that, thought the Master wryly.
'Perhaps,' he said.

The Castellan was busy at the controls of the
transmat booth. 'It is time to go.'

The Master rose and crossed to the booth, and the
Castellan gave him a flat metallic disc with a button
set into the centre. 'When you have learned something
worth telling us, activate this. We'll pick up your
signal and transmat you back.'

The Master took the recall device and put it away.
He looked round the little group. 'Isn't anyone going
to wish me luck?'

Borusa replied coldly. 'Naturally, we wish you
success. For all our sakes.'

The Master smiled cynically, and stepped into the
booth.

As if afraid that he would change his mind, the
Castellan operated the transmat controls with impatient speed. In a matter of seconds the Master faded
away. The Castellan stepped back. 'And now, we
wait, my Lord President.'

'I should prefer to wait alone.'

Accepting the dismissal, the Castellan and Chancellor Flavia went silently from the conference room.

Somewhere in the Death Zone, the Master blinked
into existence. He stood on a little knoll, surveying the
forbidden landscape around him with marked displea-
sure. Thunder rumbled, and lightning bolts flashed
across the sky. The Death Zone. A place known to
every Time Lord, but never mentioned, never visited.
Closed off, forbidden, sealed behind an impenetrable
forcefield from the rest of Gallifrey. Custodian of the

Dark Tower – and of the most horrifying secret in Time Lord history.

The Master looked around him, at mist-covered barren wasteland stretching as far as the eye could see. Over there in the distance loomed the mountains and the Tower.

The Master took a few steps forwards and his foot struck against something dry and brittle. Glancing down, he saw what appeared to be a large charred log. The Master frowned, and bent to look at it. On closer examination, the burnt log turned out to be a corpse, twisted and blackened, white teeth gleaming from the blackened skull. 'One of my predecessors!'

Charred by what, the Master wondered – and found his answer when a vicious lightning bolt sizzled from the sky towards him. Warned by some instinct, the Master flung himself aside. The bolt struck the corpse, making it dance and twitch in a ghastly parody of life. The Master regarded the grisly sight unmoved.

'Not the most hospitable of environments,' he observed thoughtfully, and hurried on his way.

The mists cleared for a moment and the Tower appeared, quite close now, surrounded by its ring of mountains. The unassuming little figure of the second Doctor stood staring up at its threatening bulk. 'You see, Brigadier, it's just as I feared. We're on Gallifrey, my home planet. In the Death Zone.'

The Brigadier frowned. 'You know this place?'

With sudden unexpected passion the Doctor shouted, 'Yes! To my shame, Brigadier.'

'*Your* shame?'

'Yes, mine, and the shame of every other Time Lord.'

51

Seeing the Brigadier's puzzled face, he went on more gently, 'In the days before Rassilon my ancestors already had tremendous powers – which they misused disgracefully. They set up this place, the Death Zone, walled it round with an impenetrable forcefield. Then they kidnapped other life forms from all over the cosmos, and set them down here.'

'What for?'

'To fight, and to die, for the amusement of the Time Lords,' said the little man. It was clear that he found the subject almost too distasteful to talk about. 'Come along, Brigadier, I'll explain as we go.'

'Where are we going?'

'To the Dark Tower, of course. To Rassilon. The greatest single figure in Time Lord history.'

The Brigadier looked up at the Tower, with a noticeable lack of enthusiasm. 'I see. And is that Tower where Rassilon lives?'

'Not exactly *lives*, Brigadier. It's his Tomb.'

A simple meal of fruit cordial and food concentrates was over, and now, watched by their companions, the two Doctors were concluding their conference.

It was a conference that looked very like turning into a quarrel.

'You're talking nonsense, my boy,' said the old man vigorously. 'What we have to do is quite clear. We must send the signal as you planned, wait for the rest of me, and then act together.'

The Doctor was equally determined. 'I'm sorry, but there simply isn't time. I'm already being affected by temporal instability. I can resist for a while, now you're here – but you know the danger?'

The old man nodded gravely. The segment of the Doctor that was trapped in the vortex was exerting a fateful pull. As next in line, this Doctor was most affected. He formed a kind of thumb in the temporal dike. If he gave way, *all* the Doctors would be swept away, dispersed in a temporal limbo.

'Even so, my boy – without our other selves, we stand little chance out there.'

'We daren't wait for the others,' said the Doctor. 'We daren't. After all, they may never make it here. There is evil at work.'

'Evil,' said Tegan. 'What kind of evil? Isn't it time we had a few explanations – such as where are we?'

Doctor One snapped, 'We're in the Death Zone on Gallifrey.'

'How do you know?'

It was the Doctor who answered, pointing to the picture of the Tower on the scanner. 'Because that's the Dark Tower. The Tomb of Rassilon.' He turned back to the old man. 'Do you really think we can afford to wait – especially if someone has tapped his power?'

'Very well. What do you intend to do, young man?'

'Go to the Tower.'

'There will be great danger.'

The Doctor nodded, accepting the risks. 'Help me to set up the computer scan. At least we can see what's out there.'

Sarah looked around her as Bessie jolted along. 'So that's why it's all so desolated!'

The third Doctor nodded. 'All this was the setting for the Game, Sarah. It's a place of evil.'

Sarah shuddered. 'It's horrible, Doctor. Kidnapping different life forms, setting them to kill each other, setting traps – and then coming to watch it all from a safe distance. It's worse than the Roman arena.'

The Doctor nodded his agreement. 'Mind you, it's all in the distant past. Old Rassilon put a stop to it in the end. Sealed off the entire Zone, forbade the use of the Timescoop. That's the way things stayed for generations – until now.'

'If the Time Lords brought you here to deal with some problem in the Zone, why don't they tell you why you're here?'

'They delight in deviousness, that's why!' said the Doctor angrily. 'It amuses them, chucking us in the deep end, watching us sink or swim.'

He stopped the car.

'Why've we stopped, Doctor?'

'Just getting my bearings.' The Doctor stood up, scanning the horizon. 'Ah yes, there it is!'

'There what is?'

The Doctor pointed and Sarah saw a tower, silhouetted in a gap between mountains. 'What is it?'

'The Tomb of Rassilon. I'm pretty sure our enemy will be using it as a base – so that's where we're going.'

'Are you sure that's a good idea, Doctor? From what you say, whatever's in that tower must have enormous powers. What can you do against them?'

The Doctor smiled down at her, his mane of white hair ruffled by the wind. 'What I've always done, Sarah Jane. Improvise!'

He sat down, gathering his cloak around him, and was just about to drive on when a black-clad figure

54

appeared, standing on a low hillock beside the road. 'Wait, Doctor!'

The newcomer was a tall man clad in black, with a neatly pointed black beard.

'Who is it, Doctor?' whispered Sarah.

'I don't know . . . it looks very like . . .'

The Doctor drove Bessie a little closer, then stopped, peering incredulously at the black-clad man on the mount. 'Jehosophat!' he said explosively. 'It really is you! I should have known you'd be behind all this!'

'Doctor, who *is* it?'

The Doctor replied, 'Allow me to introduce my best enemy, Sarah. He likes to be known as the Master!'

6

Above, Between, Below!

The third Doctor stared thoughtfully at his old enemy.
'My, my, my, you've changed! Another regeneration?'
　'Not exactly.'
　'I take it you're responsible for our presence in the
Death Zone?'
　'No, Doctor, for once I'm innocent, here at the High
Council's request – to help you, and your other selves.'
　The Doctor exploded with laughter. '*You?* Sent here,
by the Time Lords, to help *me?* I never heard such
arrant nonsense.'
　'I happen to be telling the truth, Doctor.' The
Master held out his hand. 'I carry the Seal of the High
Council.'
　The Doctor glanced briefly at the Seal. 'Forged, no
doubt.'
　'Geniune, Doctor. See for yourself.'
　The Master tossed the Seal and the Doctor caught
it. He examined the device with a puzzled frown. It
was undoubtedly genuine. The Doctor's face cleared.
　'Stolen, then,' he said cheerfully, and slipped the
Seal into his pocket. 'I'll return it at the first oppor-
tunity.
　'Doctor, if you will only listen! I'm here to help you.'

'You help me? Rubbish! This is some kind of trap.'

'I knew this was going to be difficult, Doctor – but I didn't realise that even you would be so stupid as to make it impossible. For the last time, I am here to help you.'

Despite the sneering words, the sincerity in the Master's voice was unmistakable. Just for a moment, the Doctor began to wonder if he was being too hasty. Could it be possible –

A thunderbolt sizzled down from the sky and the Master's hillock exploded in flames.

'I knew it!' yelled the Doctor. 'A trap!'

He threw the little car into a racing start, swinging around the Master and heading off into the distance. The Master's despairing voice called out behind them. 'Doctor, wait! Those thunderbolts are everywhere in the Zone . . .'

Sarah turned and saw another thunderbolt strike the ground close to the Master, blowing him off his feet. She saw him roll over, scramble to his feet and run for cover. Sarah frowned. If the thunderbolts were attacking the Master as well . . . 'Doctor, wait! Suppose you're wrong? We can't just leave him.'

'Just watch me!'

Suddenly a thunderbolt struck the rear of the car, exploding one of the back tyres, and the car screeched to a halt.

'You see,' said the Doctor triumphantly. 'What did I tell you? A trap! Come on Sarah Jane, run for it!'

They set off towards the mountains.

There was a picture of the Tower on the TARDIS console screen, but it was a computer graphics picture showing the whole of the Tower and a proportion of the countryside around it. Mysterious symbols flowed across the screen, and it seemed that this computer-scan provided the two Doctors with a great deal of useful information.

'As far as I can make out,' said the Doctor, 'there are three possible ways in. From above – climb the mountain and somehow cross to the Tower.' He pointed to the base of the picture. 'From below – there seems to be some kind of cave system.' The Doctor pointed a little higher. 'Or there's the main door – here!'

The old man nodded. 'And which approach do *you* plan to use?'

'The main door. The nearest and the simplest.'

'And very possibly the most dangerous! I still think you should wait.'

'I daren't. Remember – there may be very little time.'

'Of course,' said the second Doctor thoughtfully, 'it's always possible that Rassilon himself could have brought us here.'

The Brigadier came to a halt, and looked disapprovingly down at him. They had been on the move for quite some time. The mountains, and the Tower, were very close – too close for the Brigadier's liking.

'Hang on a minute, Doctor. You did say this chap Rassilon was dead, didn't you?' He pointed up at the Tower. 'You said *that* was his tomb.'

'Oh yes, it is,' said the little man innocently. 'But there are all sorts of legends about Rassilon you know. No one knows how extensive his powers really were.'

58

The Doctor lowered his voice. 'Some say he never really died at all!'

'He could still be alive then?'

'Watching us – at this very moment.'

The Brigadier looked round uneasily. 'Still, didn't you say Rassilon was supposed to be rather a good type?'

'So the official history tells us. But there are many rumours, many legends to the contrary. Some say Rassilon was really a cruel and bloodthirsty tyrant. Far from banning the Game, Rassilon really invented it. In that particular version of the legend, his fellow Time Lords are supposed to have rebelled against his cruelty and locked him in the Tower bound in eternal sleep.'

'So you think he's woken up again, getting up to his old tricks?'

'It would certainly explain a great deal.' The Doctor looked alarmed. 'Oh dear! We could be playing the Game of Rassilon at this very moment!'

'Your tone doesn't inspire confidence, Doctor,' said the Brigadier dryly. 'I take it we're not expected to win?'

The Doctor didn't answer.

'Come along, Brigadier,' he said at last.

They moved on, towards the Dark Tower.

The distorted faces of the fourth Doctor and his companion, the Lady Romana, swirled and twisted endlessly on the screen in the conference room. A young Time Technician, an eminent Time Lord scientist in his own right, was reporting to the Inner Council. Borusa nodded at the figures on the screen. 'You can do nothing to retrieve him?'

'Nothing, my Lord President. With the existing energy-drain from the Death Zone, it is beyond our resources!'

'We must do something,' protested Chancellor Flavia. 'As long as *he* is trapped, all the Doctors are endangered.'

Borusa considered for a moment. 'Use whatever energy you can spare to stabilise that portion of the vortex. At least that will give the remaining Doctors a little more time.'

'Lord President.' The scientist bowed and withdrew.

The Castellan joined the conference. 'I take it there is no news from the Master?'

Borusa gave him a scornful glance. 'Did you really think there would be?'

It seemed to Turlough, who had a strong streak of caution, that the Doctor was proposing to risk his life for no good reason. And if anything happened to the Doctor, things would look bad for Turlough as well. 'Even if you reach the Tower, Doctor, what are you going to do?'

'Release the TARDIS, for a start.'

Doctor One nodded towards the scanner. 'The computer scan has located the generator of the force-field paralysing the TARDIS, young man. Not surprisingly, the generator is located in the Tower, very close to the Tomb itself.'

The Doctor said, 'Well, I'd better be off.'

It had already been established that the old man would stay in the TARDIS, following the Doctor's progress on the scanner.

As the Doctor headed for the door, Tegan said, 'Wait. I'll come with you.'

Susan said, 'I'd like to come too.'

Turlough said nothing.

The Doctor looked questioningly at his other self. The old man frowned. 'It would be safer if you both remained here with me.'

'I want to come,' said Tegan determinedly.

Susan said, 'Me too!'

'Oh, very well,' said the Doctor. He looked at the old man. 'And you'll bring the TARDIS to the Tower the moment I've switched off the forcefield.'

'Of course, my boy!'

The Doctor braced himself. 'Then we'd better get started. Time is running out.'

Meanwhile Sarah and the third Doctor were toiling up a mountain path which wound steeply, and apparently endlessly, upwards.

'I thought we were going to the Tower,' protested Sarah.

The Doctor stopped, his cloak blowing in the chill mountain wind. 'We are.'

'Then why are we going this way?'

'Because', said the Doctor patiently, 'the mountains happen to be between us and the Tower. That's why.'

'Can't we find an easier route?'

'It would take far too long – besides . . .' The Doctor pointed.

Sarah looked. At the foot of the mountain, far, far below them, a group of tall silver figures was moving after them.

'It seems that the Master has used the Timescoop to

bring others here as well as us,' said the Doctor sombrely.

Sarah was still not sure that the Doctor's theory about the Master was correct. But there was no doubt at all about the group of Cybermen moving purposefully after them. Wearily she resumed her climb.

Left with nothing to do but wait, Turlough and the first Doctor were hovering anxiously over the scanner. A small point of light represented the Doctor and, presumably, his two companions. It seemed to be moving with agonising slowness. Turlough kept moving away from the screen, and then coming impatiently back to it. 'Do you think it will take them very much longer to reach the Tower?'

'Depends on what may try to stop them, my boy. It's not called the Death Zone without reason, you know.' Suddenly the old man leaned forward excitedly. 'Great Heavens! Two more traces.'

'Two more Time Lords?'

'Two more Doctors,' said the old man triumphantly. 'The scanner-trace is keyed to my – our – brain-patterns. Well, well, well, so two of them made it! I wonder what happened to the other one . . .'

The Brigadier and the second Doctor had reached the very base of the mountains by now. The ground sloped sharply upwards above them. Shading his eyes, the Brigadier could see nothing ahead but a very nasty, and very dangerous climb. Then he heard a strange, plaintive sound.

The Doctor was singing in a high quavery voice.

'Who unto Rassilon's Tower would go,' he warbled. 'Must choose – Above, Between, Below!'

'Are you in pain, Doctor?' enquired the Brigadier sarcastically.

The Doctor looked offended. 'I see that age has not mellowed you, Brigadier. I was recalling, in point of fact, an old Gallifreyan nursery rhyme – about the Dark Tower.'

'I see. Does it help?'

'Considerably more than you do! It describes three different ways to enter the Dark Tower.'

'You mean we're going to be guided by a nursery rhyme? I've never heard anything so ridiculous.'

'Nevertheless, Brigadier, I propose to put the matter to the test. And I choose – Below! Come along!'

'Come along where?'

The Doctor led the way to a cave mouth so tiny that the Brigadier hadn't even registered it.

'Down here,' said the Doctor, and popped into the tiny opening like a rabbit down a hole.

Groaning, the Brigadier squeezed through after him.

7

The Doctor Disappears

The Doctor, Tegan and Susan were hurrying over the rocky ground, heading towards the Tower. The Doctor was setting a tremendous pace. Tegan guessed he was haunted by the fear that temporal instability would set in again before he could complete his task. It must be very worrying, she thought, wondering if you were suddenly going to fade away.

Susan was struggling on bravely. After years of quiet, domestic life she found she was enjoying the adventure. 'I'm finding this quite exhilarating!'

Tegan had had more than her fair share of adventure in recent years. 'Oh, are you? I wish I was!'

The ground was beginning to fall away a little before them, descending into a kind of shallow valley which ran between them and the Tower, when a familiar black-clad figure appeared at the foot of the path ahead.

'The Master!' gasped Tegan.

'Wait here,' ordered the Doctor.

He began moving down the path towards the Master. They met in the centre of the little valley. The Doctor stopped when he felt he was near enough to talk, but still far enough from the Master for safety.

He stood waiting, forcing the Master to speak first. The Master's voice was almost diffident. 'I know this is hard to believe, Doctor, but for once I mean you no harm.'

The Doctor said lightly, 'Wasn't it Alice who was told to believe three impossible things before breakfast? Go on.'

The Master drew a deep breath. 'I have been sent here by the High Council of the Time Lords – to help you.'

From their vantage-point on the high ground, Tegan could see the Master talking earnestly. She could even hear the rumble of his voice though she was too far away to make out what was actually being said.

If Tegan was suspicious, Susan was baffled. 'Is that man a friend of the Doctor – Doctors?'

'Anything but!'

'They're talking as if they were old friends.'

'I know,' said Tegan tersely. 'That's what worries me.'

At a point beyond the valley, out of sight of both Tegan and Susan, a group of silver figures were waiting in ambush. They were extremely tall, humanoid in shape with terrifyingly blank faces, small round eyes and slits for mouths. Two handle-like projections took the place of ears, and a complicated chest-unit occupied the front of the massive bodies. Human, or at least humanoid in origin, their bodies were part organic, but mostly metal and plastic. Immensely strong, they were passionless, emotionless, tireless, and almost invulnerable, interested only in power and in conquest.

They were Cybermen.

The Cyber Lieutenant was reporting to his Leader. 'Two aliens have been detected climbing the mountain. A patrol has been despatched in pursuit. We have located the party from the TARDIS. They have reached the valley close by. They have joined forces with another alien. Shall I take the patrol and destroy them?'

The Cyberleader considered. 'Capture them alive. They must be interrogated before they are destroyed.'

'Yes, Leader.'

'Remember also that we will need the Time Lord to pilot the TARDIS. Now go.'

The Cyber Lieutenant turned and stalked over to the group of waiting Cybermen. 'Here are your orders.'

The Cyberleader watched as the little group moved away. Things were going well.

He was uncertain as to how he and his troops came to be in this strange place, but that was unimportant. Now that they were here, they would act in a way that befitted Cybermen. They would conquer, destroying all opposition.

The Master had talked himself almost hoarse. Still the Doctor listened with that same infuriating air of silent scepticism. 'Be reasonable, Doctor!'

'I am. I'm listening.'

The Master changed his tactics, producing his Tissue Compression Eliminator, a hideous weapon that left only a tiny shrunken corpse. 'As you see, I am armed. I could kill you easily – if I wanted to.'

'Just like that – without humiliating me first?' The Doctor shook his head. 'Not your style at all.'

The Master took out the recall device and held it out. 'I also have this — a recall device that will take me back to the Inner Council's conference room in the heart of the Capitol.'

'So you say,' said the Doctor infuriatingly. 'I would prefer something more positive in the way of credentials.'

'Not long ago I had the Seal of the High Council,' said the Master bitterly.

'Then where is it?'

'One of your other selves took it from me.'

'All in all you really have told me the most fantastic tale,' said the Doctor thoughtfully. 'Do you expect me to believe it, I wonder? Or have you some other reason for delaying me here?'

Giant silver figures appeared on the skyline. Engrossed in their conversation, neither of the adversaries saw them. But Tegan did. Jumping to her feet she yelled, 'Doctor, look out! Cybermen!'

The Doctor cupped his hands to his lips. 'Go back!'

Susan looked in anguish at Tegan. 'We can't just leave him!'

'We can't help him either,' said Tegan practically. 'Come on, do as he says. We must warn the others.'

She began heading back to the TARDIS. Susan started to follow but she couldn't resist turning back to see what was happening . . .

The Doctor and the Master were both running by now, trying to evade a rapidly-closing circle of Cybermen. There seemed to be only one gap in the ring and naturally enough they found themselves both running towards it, almost bumping into each other. 'After you,' said the Doctor politely.

The Master sprinted ahead.

'Halt, or you will be destroyed,' roared the Cyber Lieutenant. He fired a warning shot. It disintegrated a rock close to the Master's fleeing figure. Fragments of rock flew through the air, and one of them took the Master on the forehead. He reeled and fell.

The Doctor ran up to him, instinctively kneeling to see if he could help. He saw the trickle of blood on the Master's forehead. 'Zapped!' He saw the recall device, in the Master's outflung hand. He looked up, and saw the ring of Cybermen closing in.

Although she knew it was almost suicidally dangerous, Susan still couldn't resist hanging back.

She saw the Master fall.

She saw the Doctor kneeling by his body.

She saw the Cybermen closing in.

Recall device in his hand, the Doctor looked up and saw the Cyber Lieutenant standing over him. The eerie mechanical voice said, 'You will accompany me.'

'Sorry, must dash,' said the Doctor.

A reddish halo surrounded his body and he faded away.

Susan looked on in astonishment, as the Doctor faded out of existence. She heard Tegan's voice. 'What are you *doing*, Susan. Come on!' She ran towards the waiting Tegan – but even as she ran she turned again to look over her shoulder. Her foot turned on a chunk

68

of loose rock and she stumbled and fell. Tegan ran back, helping Susan to her feet. 'Can you walk?'

'Just about . . .'

'Then get moving. Here, let me help you.'

Her arm round Tegan's shoulders, Susan hobbled away.

A figure materialised in the haze of light in the transmat booth. The Doctor stepped out and glanced around the table. President Borusa, Chancellor Flavia and the Castellan gazed at him in blank astonishment.

'Well, well,' said the Doctor. 'Quite a reception committee!'

The Master recovered consciousness, stabbing frantically at the button on the recall device – until he realised it was no longer in his hand. Looking up, he saw himself surrounded by a ring of Cybermen.

The Cyberleader approached and studied the Master. 'This is not the Doctor.'

The Master scrambled to his feet, brushing himself down. 'I'm glad you're here at last,' he said calmly. 'I've been looking for you.'

'Kill him,' said the Cyberleader.

The Cybermen raised their weapons.

The Master shouted, 'Wait! I am here as your friend. I can help you.'

The Cyberleader raised a hand to check his men. 'Who are you?'

The Master bowed. 'The Master – and your loyal servant.'

*

Back in the TARDIS, Tegan was binding Susan's ankle. Susan was telling the first Doctor the story of their ill-fated expedition. 'Then the Doctor just disappeared,' she concluded.

'Vanished?' said Turlough. 'How? What could have happened?'

'From the way Susan described it, young man,' snapped the first Doctor, 'Through the operation of some kind of transmat device.'

Tegan said, 'But the Doctor didn't . . . of course! He must have got it from the Master. Thing is, where did it take him?'

Susan shook her head. 'No idea. I just hope he's all right.'

The first Doctor drew himself up. 'Well, wherever our young friend may have got to – *I* shall have to go to the Dark Tower!'

The old boy might be tetchy and domineering, thought Tegan, but you had to admire his spirit.

'Good for you,' she said. 'I'll come with you.'

The old man actually smiled. 'Thank you, my dear.'

The Doctor had given a brief report on his adventures to the Inner Council. Now he was listening to the Castellan's account of recent events on Gallifrey – the re-activation of the Death Zone, the energy-drain from the Eye of Harmony, the abduction of his other selves. Finally, the decision to despatch the Master as an agent of the Council. A decision which the Castellan freely admitted had been taken against President Borusa's advice.

When the Castellan had finished, the Doctor said, 'It seems I have done the Master an injustice.'

'Should he survive, I'm sure he will learn to live with your misjudgement,' said Borusa.

'This changes things,' the Doctor went on. 'If the Master isn't responsible – then who *is* misusing the Death Zone?'

The Castellan said, 'We were hoping you could tell us that, Doctor. After all, you have just been there.'

'Who has control of the Timescoop?'

'No one,' said Borusa crisply. 'Its use has long been prohibited.'

'But the machinery still exists?'

Borusa shrugged. 'Presumably. It has been unused so long that even the location of the Game control room is now unknown.'

'Not presumably to everyone!'

'You seemed to be implying that the Timescoop was used to bring you here?' said Borusa coldly.

'Yes, I am rather.'

Chancellor Flavia looked keenly at him. 'Then since the machinery, *if* it still exists, is somewhere here, in the Capitol – you accuse a Time Lord?'

'Yes. I should think it would be quite an important one as well. Probably one of the High Council.'

Borusa sat back in his Presidential chair. 'You have evidence, of course, Doctor?'

'Not yet.'

'Then on what do you base this outrageous accusation?'

'This and that,' said the Doctor vaguely. 'I thought at first someone was simply trying to revive the Game. But then, there are the Cybermen ... Whoever brought me and my other selves here, brought them as well. You know the legends well enough. Even in our most corrupt period, our ancestors never allowed the Cybermen to play the Game. Like the Daleks, they fight too well. Yet the Cybermen are in the Zone – and a Dalek too, I gather.'

The Castellan leaned forward angrily. 'You admit then that you have no proof that there is a traitor on the High Council?'

'Well, there's this,' said the Doctor mildly. He held out the recall device. 'The Death Zone is a very big place, yet the Cybermen found us very quickly. Almost as if they were supposed to.'

'They are highly skilled in such matters,' said Borusa wearily.

'Especially when helped?' The Doctor held up the device. 'Remember, this is the one thing the Master would be sure to keep on him at all times.' The Doctor took a penknife from his pocket and prised off the base plate of the device, revealing a small brightly pulsing light. 'A powerful homing device – transmitting a signal that would easily be picked up by Cybermen ground-scanners.'

Borusa leaned forward, fixing the Castellan with his piercing gaze. 'A homing device . . . which you gave him, Castellan!'

8

Condemned

The Castellan leaped to his feet. 'It's a lie! The Doctor is after revenge.' He was referring to an occasion, not so very long ago, when with the best possible motives the Castellan had been instrumental in having the Doctor sentenced to death.

'Sit down, Castellan,' said Borusa coldly.

'I will not submit to these wild accusations.'

'Sit down.'

Trembling with rage, the Castellan resumed his seat.

Borusa touched the control in his chair arm, and a burly Guard Commander appeared. The Commander crashed to attention. 'Lord President?'

'You will institute an immediate and rigorous search of the offices and living quarters of the Castellan.' The Commander wheeled and stamped away.

The Castellan sat staring ahead of him, his face a ghastly white. He looked, thought the Doctor, like a man condemned to death.

In the hollow that the Cybermen used as their base, the Master stood before the Cyberleader. He was talking for his life.

'I do not believe your lies,' said the Cyberleader flatly.

'What I have told you is the truth. Do you know how you come to be here? Do you?' There was no reply. The Master smiled triumphantly. 'You were brought here, just as I was. We've all been brought here, and for the same reason.'

'To fight?'

'To fight and die, for the amusement of the Time Lords.' The Master leaned forward urgently. 'But you don't have to play their game. You can defeat them, gain your revenge – but only with my help!'

'Explain.'

'You have seen the Tower, close by? It is a fortress. The fortress of your enemies – the Time Lords. It is well defended, but I can help you to conquer it.'

'What do you ask in return?'

The Master shrugged. 'My life. My freedom. A chance to share in your revenge – to destroy the Time Lords.'

The Cyberleader gestured to one of his troops. 'Guard him.'

The Cyberleader moved a little apart, and his Lieutenant followed.

'You will send a patrol to capture the TARDIS,' ordered the Cyberleader. 'The remaining patrol will go with the Master to the Tower.'

'He is an Alien. Aliens are not to be trusted.'

'It is not necessary to trust him.'

'Will you give him his freedom?'

The Cyberleader said, 'Promises made to Aliens have no validity. Once the Tower is in our hands he will be destroyed.'

The Cyberleader turned and strode back to the Master. 'You will guide us to the Tower!' Well satisfied, the Master smiled and bowed. He had told the Cybermen a carefully simplified story – by now the Master too was convinced that something far more complex was going on than a simple revival of the Game. The truth, whatever it was, lay in the Tower.

Now it was Susan and Turlough who stood peering into the scanner, tracing the tiny dot that registered the first Doctor's progress.

'They're moving so slowly,' said Susan.

Turlough shrugged. 'Don't worry. Tegan will look after the old man.'

Suddenly they heard a scuffling sound from outside. A great thump shook the TARDIS. Hurriedly Turlough switched the scanner back on to normal picture. The screen was filled with giant silver shapes.

'Oh no,' gasped Susan. 'Cybermen!'

To the Brigadier's surprise, the little cave mouth led into a narrow tunnel – a tunnel that seemed to wind steadily upwards. Unfortunately the tunnel was narrow and low-ceilinged. It served well enough for a little chap like the Doctor, but a man of the Brigadier's impressive bulk had to move along it doubled up like a hoop, cursing his aching back, and scraping knees and elbows. The Brigadier struggled on, infuriated more than encouraged by the cheerful voice ahead of him.

'Come along, Brigadier. Come along. This way! Mind your head!'

Cursing, the Brigadier struggled through a particularly narrow gap to find the Doctor waiting for him in a slightly wider section. 'Dammit, Doctor, I'm just not built for this kind of thing any more.'

'You never were,' said the Doctor unkindly. 'Cheer up – we're getting along very nicely. The tunnel's rising all the time. We should be at the Tower very soon.'

'Is that supposed to cheer me up?'

A low, sinister growling came out of the darkness behind them.

The Brigadier spun round. 'What was that?'

There came another scraping, shuffling sound. Then a bloodthirsty growl. The Doctor said thoughtfully, 'It sounded to me like something very large, very fierce and probably very hungry. Come on, Brigadier – run!'

High up on the mountain path, Sarah and the third Doctor found themselves facing a dead end. The path ran between high rock walls and disappeared into a cave. Before the cave a wider, flatter area, strewn with rocks and giant boulders, made a sort of pass.

'It's a dead end,' said Sarah despairingly.

The Doctor shook his head. 'No it's not. It's a pass. Look!'

Just beyond the cave was the beginning of an incredibly steep and narrow path that seemed to wind up to the summit.

'I couldn't go up there,' protested Sarah. 'I'll get vertigo.'

'Don't worry, I'll help you!'

Sarah wasn't convinced. 'Let's just go back, Doctor, for an easier way.'

'We can't go back.'

'Why not? We seem to have shaken off the Cyber-men.'

'No we haven't. Cybermen don't shake off. They never get tired and they never give up!'

'All right, all right, I remember,' said Sarah wearily. 'Okay, let's go then. If I don't fall off that path, I'll probably die of fright anyway.'

She was about to move forward when an astonishing sight appeared in the cave mouth. It was some kind of robot. Basically man-shaped and very tall and thin, it had a smooth, shining body surface in gleaming metal. Its head was completely blank, a metal egg, with no eyes or mouth. Its movements were lithe and graceful, like those of a trained athlete.

'What is it?' whispered Sarah.

'A Raston Warrior Robot – the most perfect killing-machine ever devised.'

'But it's not armed.'

Sarah must have spoken a fraction too loudly. The Robot wheeled round in her direction. One hand went back over its shoulder and then flashed forwards. A thin steel rod, like a javelin, flashed through the air and stuck quivering at Sarah's feet.

'Quick, over there,' whispered the Doctor. He dragged her behind the shelter of another boulder. Lips close to her ear he whispered, 'The armaments are built in and the sensors detect movement. Any movement.'

'Anything else I shouldn't like to know,' whispered Sarah.

'Yes,' the Doctor whispered. 'It can move like – '

The Robot blurred and vanished.

'Lightning,' concluded the Doctor.

They looked cautiously around, and saw the Robot standing quite motionless among the rocks, some way behind them.

The Doctor and Sarah ducked down.

'What's it doing?' whispered Sarah.

The Doctor said, 'It's playing with us.'

Slowly, very slowly, they moved into cover. 'Freeze, Sarah Jane,' whispered the Doctor. 'If we move – we're dead.'

Susan and Turlough staggered as the TARDIS shook and rocked under the repeated hammering of giant metal fists. The noise was deafening.

'If only we could get away from here,' muttered Turlough. He looked accusingly at Susan. 'You told me you travelled with the Doctor for ages. Can't you operate the controls?'

'You forget – the TARDIS is paralysed. We're still trapped by the forcefield from the Tower. We can't move till the Doctor neutralises it.'

Tegan and the first Doctor were very close to the Tower now, but the going was rough, and Tegan had to give the old man quite a lot of help.

'Come on, Doc, you can make it,' she said encouragingly.

The old man scowled at her. 'Of course I can, young woman. And kindly refrain from addressing me as Doc!'

They struggled on.

The Guard Commander put an ornately-decorated metal casket on the conference room table, and stepped back as if he was afraid it might contaminate him.

'This is the casket, Lord President. As you see, it bears the Seal of Rassilon.'

Borusa nodded. 'And where did you find it?'

'In the Castellan's room – well hidden.'

Carefully Borusa opened the lid. The casket was filled with rolled parchment scrolls, bound with black silk ribbon, sealed with the same seal that was on the casket. Chancellor Flavia drew back in horror. 'The Black Scrolls of Rassilon! This is forbidden knowledge!'

'How very interesting,' said the Doctor. 'I thought they were out of print!' He reached for the casket, but Borusa snatched it away, slamming shut the lid.

'No, Doctor. This is forbidden knowledge, from the Dark Times.'

The Doctor was the first to notice the faint wisp of smoke coming from the casket. Before he could even shout a warning the wisp became a black plume, the plume became a stream and suddenly something inside the casket flared white and exploded.

When the smoke cleared, Borusa lifted the lid. The Black Scrolls had been totally incinerated, leaving nothing but a box of fine ash. Borusa turned his cold gaze on the Castellan. 'You were taking no chances.'

The Castellan licked dry lips. 'I am innocent. I have never seen that casket before.'

Borusa nodded to the Guard Commander. 'Take him to Security and get the truth out of him.' The Commander put a hand on the Castellan's shoulder. Numbly he rose and allowed himself to be led away. As he reached the door, Borusa called, 'Commander! You are authorised to use the mind probe.' The

Castellan shouted, 'No!' but the protest was quelled and the guards dragged him roughly away.

The Doctor shuddered. The mind probe worked quickly, or not at all. Resist too long and you were left a mindless idiot. 'Let me speak to him. Perhaps I can persuade – '

Borusa shook his head. 'The mind probe will provide us with all the answers we require.'

Suddenly there was an outbreak of shouting from the corridor outside. They heard sounds of struggle and the unmistakable crack of a staser blast. The Doctor leaped up and ran out into the corridor. There he saw a kind of frozen tableau. The Castellan lay face down some little way along the corridor. A blaster lay close to his outstretched hand. The Commander was standing over him – reholstering his phaser. Nearby the other guards stood frozen like waxworks.

The Doctor looked down at the Castellan's body, then up at the Commander. 'Was that necessary?'

'He was armed,' said the Commander impassively. 'Armed, and trying to escape.'

The Doctor turned and went back into the conference room. No one seemed to have moved since he had left. The Doctor dropped wearily into a chair. 'It seems you have been saved the embarrassment of a trial, Lord President.'

'And you have found your traitor, Doctor,' said Borusa. 'We can only hope that the task of your other selves will now be simplified.'

The Doctor rose. 'I'd better be getting back to them.' He moved towards the transmat booth.

'No, Doctor,' said Borusa firmly. 'I admire your

courage, but I cannot allow you to return. I still need your help and advice.'

'But my companions are in the Death Zone. I can't abandon them.'

'I am sure your other selves will be able to cope.'

'Are they all in the Zone?'

'All but one!' Borusa touched a control and the distorted features of the fourth Doctor and Romana appeared on the screen. 'As you see, he is trapped in the vortex.' The screen went dark. 'I am sorry, Doctor, but I must insist that you remain here in the Capitol. Chancellor Flavia, perhaps you would escort the Doctor to a place of rest. I'm sure he must be exhausted.'

'Of course. If you will accompany me, Doctor?'

Chancellor Flavia led the Doctor from the conference room.

The second Doctor and the Brigadier hurried along the tunnels, the snuffling, grunting and roaring of the creature very close behind them.

'Whatever that thing is, Doctor,' panted the Brigadier, 'it's got our scent now. It's *hunting* us.'

The Doctor saw a small opening in the tunnel wall and nipped inside. 'Quick, Brigadier. In here.'

The Doctor had slipped through the gap, and the Brigadier, with a good deal more effort, squeezed through after him. They found themselves in a tiny cave, just big enough to hold them both. There was a shattering roar from outside, and something very large hurled itself against the gap through which they'd come. Luckily it was much too large, its massive bulk filling the gap.

'It's all right,' said the Doctor. 'It can't get in. It's much too big!'

'Maybe it can't get in,' said the Brigadier, 'but we can't get out. It's got us trapped!'

9

The Dark Tower

The little Doctor stood quite still for a moment, considering the situation. He began searching frantically through his pockets. 'There must be something useful here . . .'

There came a fierce scrabbling from outside, and the rattle of falling rock. Either the local stone was exceptionally soft or the creature outside was quite inconceivably strong.

'Better hurry, Doctor,' said the Brigadier. 'It's trying to dig us out!'

'Aha!' said the Doctor triumphantly. 'Here we are!' There was a slender tube-shaped object in his hand. 'Have you got a light, Brigadier?' The Brigadier fished a lighter out of his pocket and handed it over. The Doctor lit the end of the tube and tossed it through the gap.

'What was that?' whispered the Brigadier. 'A bomb?'

'A Giant Galactic Glitter!'

'Well, it doesn't seem to be working.'

'Wait!'

Suddenly a fountain of golden sparks shot up in the air outside the little cave, illuminating in its golden glow the giant shaggy form of the creature that was pursuing them.

'It's a Yeti!' said the Doctor happily. He sounded almost as if he was welcoming an old friend. The Brigadier shuddered, remembering the days when the shaggy robot-beasts had terrorised London. It was then that he had first met the Doctor. 'Where did it come from?'

The Doctor shrugged. 'Left over from the Game perhaps. Or maybe it was brought here for our benefit.'

The shower of sparks ended in a very loud bang – and an even louder roar of rage from the Yeti.

'You've maddened it!' shouted the Brigadier.

Scrabbling claws appeared in the gap and the whole cave seemed to shudder as the monster hurled itself against the rock wall, followed by the rumbling sound of a rock fall. The creature must have dislodged loose rock, somewhere up above. The Doctor and the Brigadier leaped back as a curtain of rock fell, blocking their escape completely.

For a moment there was only silence and darkness. The Brigadier snapped on his lighter. The flame flared high, revealing the rock pile blocking the entrance, and the guilty face of the Doctor. He looked apologetically at the Brigadier. 'Well, at least the Yeti can't get at us now.'

'We're trapped,' said the Brigadier grimly. 'Buried alive.'

The Doctor stared worriedly at the lighter flame. 'Yes, I'm afraid we are . . .'

The flame flickered wildly and almost went out. It recovered, but it was still streaming over to one side.

The Doctor said, 'On the other hand – where there's a wind, there's a way!' He scrabbled his way to the back of the little cave and called 'Over here, Brigadier. There's another gap!'

And so there was. They crawled through it and up into a still narrower tunnel, sloping even more steeply upwards.

'Well, well,' said the Doctor suddenly. 'I think we've arrived.'

He pointed ahead. The tunnel ended suddenly in a smooth stone wall, into which there was set a small metal door. The Brigadier gave the door a tentative push. To his surprise, it swung smoothly open. The Doctor frowned. 'I don't like that. I don't like that at all.'

'Why not?'

'Someone or something *wants* us to go inside. After you, Brigadier.'

'No, Doctor,' said the Brigadier, with equal politeness. 'After you!'

Turlough adjusted the scanner lens, trying to follow the movements of the little group of Cybermen moving about outside the TARDIS. Susan was doing her best to be cheerful.

'Well, at least that terrible banging's stopped.'

'That's what worries me,' said Turlough gloomily. He peered up at the screen. The Cybermen appeared to be bringing up some kind of device. Something metallic, and very large.

'What's that they're carrying?' asked Susan. 'What are they planning to do?'

Turlough said wearily, 'Well I don't actually *know*.

But I would think their intention is to break in — wouldn't you?'

The end of Sarah's nose itched. She had agonising cramp in her left toe. She shifted her position ever so slightly, and the tall silver figure of the Robot swung round. Sarah froze again.

'I can't take much more of this!'

The tall, white-haired figure of the third Doctor might have been carved from solid rock. Even when he spoke, his lips didn't move. 'Hang on, Sarah Jane. Hang on. I think we've got just one hope.'

'What?'

The Doctor drew in his breath. 'Look, Sarah. Here it comes!'

A Cyberman stalked arrogantly into the space before the cave. The Cyber patrol had caught up with them. The Cyberman stared at the Robot, raised its weapon — and was immediately transfixed with a metal lance. This time there was a slender thread attached to the lance. The Cyberman staggered, and raised its weapon again. The Robot twitched the thread and the Cyberman crashed to the ground. It staggered to its feet and advanced once more. The Robot blurred, reappeared in a different position and hurled a silver disc which sliced the Cyberman's head from its body. The headless Cyberman staggered a few steps, firing wildly, and crashed to the ground.

More Cybermen came pouring into the pass. The first of them raised his weapon. A silver disc sliced his arm from his body. The arm fell, the weapon still firing. The Cybermen crowded closer, trying to surround the Robot. They never stood a chance. The

Robot blurred and reappeared changing its position every time a Cyberman fired. It sliced off arms and legs and heads with silver discs, sending Cybermen reeling to the ground. It transfixed them with steel lances, and enmeshed them in fine metallic thread. If a Cyberman came too close, the Robot extruded a sword-blade from its hand and sliced it to pieces.

The Doctor and Sarah watched the massacre with fascinated horror. It was hard to feel sorry for a Cyberman, but Sarah found herself watching the slaughter of the silver giants with something very like pity. Before the flashing quicksilver movements of the Robot they were clumsy and helpless. When the battle was at its height, the Doctor tapped her shoulder. 'Come on, Sarah Jane. Now's our chance.' They ran round the edge of the battle and headed up the narrow path.

A Cyberman, wounded and weaponless, saw their escape and staggered determinedly after them.

As they hurried up the precipitous mountain path, the Doctor paused for a moment.

Stacked neatly against the rock wall was some of the Robot's spare equipment: steel lances, razor-edged throwing discs, and coils of metallic thread. The Doctor grabbed a handful of lances. 'At least we'll have something to fight with. Hang on a minute, this might come in handy as well.' He snatched up several coils of metallic thread and hurried after Sarah.

As the Doctor turned a corner and disappeared, the wounded Cyberman came staggering up the path after him.

*

By now only one Cyberman was still on its feet, facing the Robot. As the Cyberman raised its weapon, the Robot flicked out its sword-blade and sliced off its arm. It blurred and shifted position, and lopped off the Cyberman's head. A series of swift flashing strokes reduced the Cyberman to scattered chunks of metal and plastic. Retracting the blade the Robot stood poised, motionless, surrounded by the bodies of its enemies.

The Doctor and Sarah struggled up the last few feet of path and found themselves on the edge of a precipice, lined with massive boulders. Looking over the edge, Sarah was astonished to see how far they had climbed. Below, very close to them, was the top of the Dark Tower, shrouded in mists.

Sarah turned to the Doctor. 'What do we do now? Fly?'

'What a splendid idea, Sarah Jane!'

Washed and brushed and wined and dined, the fifth Doctor was his usual neat self again. Nevertheless, his face was sombre and preoccupied as he strolled along the corridors of the Capitol beside Chancellor Flavia. Noticing his expression, Chancellor Flavia came to a halt. 'You look worried, Doctor,' she said. 'Your friends and your other selves will come safely through their dangers, I am sure.'

'At the moment I'm almost more concerned for the High Council, and for Gallifrey.'

'Surely, the traitor has been found?'

'Has he? I've known the Castellan for a very long time. He was limited, a little narrow, and ruthless when he thought it his duty. But he was always fiercely loyal to his oath of office. Any mention of the Dark Days, of the Forbidden Knowledge, filled him with horror. You saw his reaction to the Black Scrolls?'

Chancellor Flavia nodded slowly.

'Not so much the reaction of a guilty man discovered,' said the Doctor. 'More sheer disbelief.'

As they walked on the Doctor said, 'I am convinced that the traitor is still at large.'

Although she could be obstinate, Chancellor Flavia was a shrewd and intelligent woman, and the Doctor had spelled out her own hidden fears. 'I agree that there is still cause for concern, Doctor. I shall speak to the Commander who killed the Castellan. I have a suspicion that there may be much to be learnt from him.

The Doctor said slowly, 'I must speak to the Lord President.'

After a few more words, they separated, going their different ways. Now it was Chancellor Flavia who looked worried.

Sarah looked on appalled as the Doctor fashioned one end of his coil of steel wire into a kind of lasso. She glanced down the steep path and saw a Cyberman lumbering towards them. 'Doctor, look out! There's a Cyberman coming.' The Doctor didn't even look up.

'See if you can hold it off, will you? I won't be a second.' Sarah gave him a withering look. Hold it off, indeed! She picked up the biggest rock she could manage, and lobbed it down the path towards the

Cyberman. Wounded as it was, it managed to step aside, and the rock rolled harmlessly by.

'I missed, Doctor!'

The Doctor finished his noose and looked up. 'What? There, that should do it.'

Sarah looked at the loop, and then down at the Tower. 'You're crazy. It'll never work!'

The Doctor looked down at the Cyberman labouring towards them. 'Maybe not. But unless you've got a better suggestion?'

Sarah hadn't.

'Right, then,' said the Doctor. 'Stand back!' Whirling the loop around his head the Doctor cast it towards the Tower. The loop dropped over one of the turrets and pulled itself tight. Following the Doctor's instructions, Sarah wrapped the other end of the metal wire around the biggest of the boulders, a massive column of rock.

The Doctor meanwhile was busily making a kind of stirrup arrangement, which he attached to the wire rope linking them to the Tower. 'It's quite simple, Sarah Jane. You put your foot in here, hold on here, jump off and away you go!'

Sarah didn't believe it for one moment. What decided her was the wounded Cyberman still lumbering to the top of the path. Luckily it seemed to have lost its weapon, but even wounded and unarmed it could tear them to pieces.

The Doctor called, 'Come on, Sarah Jane.' He put his foot in his stirrup, held on tight and leaped into space.

Numb with terror, Sarah did the same. She found herself flying through the foggy air at terrifying speed.

90

The Cyberman grabbed at her, missed, staggered and almost fell. Determined to the last it struggled to the boulder and tried to unfasten the rope. Its strength gave out at last and it fell dying at the foot of the boulder.

Leading his new-found allies to the Tower, the Master glanced casually upwards – and saw the Doctor and Sarah apparently flying through the air. The Master smiled. 'Ever resourceful, Doctor.'

Looking back, he saw the Cybermen too were gazing upwards in astonishment. Seizing his chance, the Master drew ahead.

The Doctor thumped onto the Tower roof, swung himself over the edge, and reached out to catch Sarah, who arrived almost on top of him. 'All right, Sarah. Hold tight. Try to find a foothold, that's right. Don't look down, I've got you.' Somehow or other he managed to heave her over the battlements. 'Well done, Sarah Jane. Enjoy the flight?'

'Great!' Sarah looked around the flat stone roof. 'All right, we're here. How do we get in?'

The Doctor searched round and spotted a ring-bolt set into the roof. He heaved on it, and found it attached to a trapdoor, which lifted smoothly upwards. 'Well, would you believe it,' said the Doctor thoughtfully. 'Come on Sarah Jane. In here!'

Tegan and the Doctor – the first Doctor – reached the Dark Tower at last. They climbed up a massive stone staircase, and found themselves facing a set of colossal doors. They were firmly closed.

'Now what?' demanded Tegan. 'You're not going to suggest we batter them down, I hope?'

The old man stood looking about him getting his breath back after the steep climb. He noticed a thick rope hanging down by the side of the doors and pottered over to examine it.

Tegan followed. 'What's that?'

'It looks very like a bell to me!'

'I suppose we just pull it and the door opens?'

'We can but try.'

The Doctor grabbed the bell-rope and gave a hefty tug.

There was a deep and sonorous clanging, which faded away into silence. Then to Tegan's utter astonishment, the doors creaked slowly open. Dwarfed by the immense size of the doors, the Doctor and Tegan went inside.

Three Doctors had entered the Dark Tower. Now the real danger would begin.

10

Deadly Companions

Outside the TARDIS, the Cybermen were busier than ever.

Susan and Turlough watched helplessly on the scanner as a group of Cybermen carried an enormous metal cylinder and set it down by the TARDIS door. Susan looked at Turlough. 'Its a bomb – isn't it?'

He nodded, making an unsuccessful attempt to sound casual 'I imagine so. Big, isn't it?'

The enormous doors gave on to an enormous hall. Tegan blinked. She had been bracing herself to meet all kinds of horrors, and instead there was – nothing. The hall was vast, cavernous and gloomy, empty except for the occasional pillar. In the distance, on the far side, she could just make out a huge staircase, leading upwards. Immediately in front of them, on the floor, alternating squares of black and white were laid out in a chess-board design.

Tegan was about to set off for the staircase when the old man put a hand on her arm. 'Don't be in such a hurry, my dear.' He fished a handful of coins from out of his pocket, oddly shaped coins from many times and many planets. Tegan looked at him in surprise. 'We have to pay to get in?'

'It could cost you your life,' said the Doctor cryptically. He tossed a coin onto the first row of the chessboard. Nothing happened.

He tossed another coin on the second row.

Still nothing.

Nothing happened on the third row, or the fourth.

Tegan was getting impatient.

'How long do you plan to stand here playing pitch and toss?'

Ignoring her, the Doctor tossed a coin onto the fifth row – and the chess-board seemed to explode. A kind of lightning bolt flashed down from the high ceiling, again and again and again, striking square after square with incredible speed. It seemed to range over the entire board, striking many, but by no means all of the squares, in turn. So, thought Tegan, some squares were safe, for some of the time – but which?

'Diabolical ingenuity,' muttered the Doctor. 'You see? Nothing happens until you reach the fifth row, half-way. Then the entire board becomes a death-trap.'

'Our ancestors had such a wonderful sense of humour,' said a smooth voice from the doorway behind them.

They turned and saw the Master striding into the hall. The first Doctor peered suspiciously at him. 'Do I know you, young man?' The Master came to join them, at the edge of the board.

'Believe it or not, we were at the Academy together.'

'What do you want?' asked Tegan suspiciously.

The Master spread his hands. 'To help.'

94

'Oh really? That's the funniest thing I've heard all day.'

'Believe what you like, but I should advise you to hide. I have some very suspicious allies close behind me.'

'Allies? What – '

She broke off as a massive silver figure loomed up in the doorway.

'Come on,' whispered Tegan. Grabbing the old Doctor's hand she dragged him behind the nearest pillar.

The Master turned towards the doorway. 'Enter – but be careful.' The Cyberleader marched into the hall, his patrol behind him. The Master waved his hand, gesturing around the vast hall. 'The fortress of the Time Lords is at your mercy.' The Cybermen gathered in the doorway, a tightly bunched, suspicious group.

The Cyber Lieutenant looked round the hall. 'Why was the main gate unguarded?'

'The Time Lords believe that no one could survive in the Death Zone. It's the kind of woolly thinking that will bring about their destruction.' The Master pointed to the great stairway at the other end of the hall. 'There lies your way!'

The Cybermen moved forward as far as the edge of the chess-board, and then stopped. The Master looked at them in surprise. 'Do you fear an empty room? Shall I lead the way?'

Tegan and the Doctor watched from hiding as the Master moved on to the board. First row, second row, third row . . . he stopped, looking expectantly at the Cybermen. The Cyberleader raised his weapon. 'You will cross to the far side.' The Master shrugged. 'Very well.'

To their astonishment he strolled across the rest of the board – though Tegan noticed he followed a slightly eccentric path, never quite moving in a straight line. On the far side of the board, the Master turned, and made the return journey. But the path he followed this time was slightly different. He returned to stand by the Cybermen. 'You see?'

The Cyberleader turned to his Lieutenant. 'Take the patrol across.' Very slowly, weapons at the ready, the giant silver figures moved across the chess-board. The Doctor and Tegan saw them reach the first square, the second, the third and the fourth . . . As the Cyberleader's foot touched the fifth row, the lightning bolts struck. Again and again and again they flashed down from the ceiling, and each time a Cyberman was struck it reeled and fell, smoke pouring from its chest-unit.

By pure chance one or two of the Cybermen survived for a time, but there was nothing they could do to fight back. They staggered disorientated about the board, firing wildly, sometimes hitting their fellows. One by one the lightning bolts found them and they were smashed burning to the ground. The Cyber Lieutenant was the last to fall. Struggling desperately to return to his Leader he was struck down at the very edge of the board. His gun skidded across the floor landing almost at the Cyberleader's feet.

The Cyberleader had watched the slaughter of his men with no apparent emotion. He turned to the Master. 'You betrayed us. Why?'

The Master looked hurt. 'Betrayed? I may have

misled you a little, unintentionally of course. You see the safe path across the board changes with every journey.'

The Cyberleader's weapon was covering the Master. 'Show me the safe route, or I shall destroy you.'

'As you wish.' The Master bowed, and suddenly converted the bow into a dive. He hit the floor, rolled over, and came up firing, the fallen Cyberweapon in his hand. Before the Cyberleader realised what was happening, the Master's first blast struck him full in the chest-unit. The Cyberleader staggered back, on to the board. The Master blasted him again and again, driving him further onto the board. Smoke pouring from his chest, the dying Cyberleader staggered on to the fifth row, triggering another sequence of the deadly lightning bolts. Seconds later, a bolt smashed him to the ground, to lie amongst the slaughtered bodies of his patrol. The Master threw back his head and laughed.

Tegan and the first Doctor came out of hiding. Tegan glared indignantly at the Master. 'Wasn't that a little ruthless, even for you?'

The Master smiled. 'In one of the many wars on your miserable little planet, they used to drive sheep across minefields. The principle is the same.'

'Not quite. This minefield is still just as dangerous.'

'You think so?'

The Master strolled across the board, apparently casually – though again, Tegan noticed, he picked his route with great care. On the other side of the board, the Master turned and waved. 'Try it, Doctor,' he invited. 'It's as easy as pie!' He turned and disappeared up the giant staircase.

The old Doctor stared after him indignantly. 'What an extraordinary fellow! Easy as pie? Easy as pie. . .'

Tegan shrugged. 'That's what he said.'

Suddenly the Doctor chuckled. 'No he didn't. He said easy as pi. Greek letter pi. Surely you know some basic mathematics, child?'

'Of course I do,' said Tegan indignantly. Closing her eyes she began reciting a long-ago lesson. '"The ratio of the circumference of a circle to its diameter is represented by the Greek letter pi."' She opened her eyes. 'Right?'

'Exactly. You work out the safe path, by using the mathematical term pi, that's clear enough. But the application, the application . . .'

The Doctor frowned, studying the board. 'A hundred squares, ten by ten . . . So, using the first hundred terms of pi as *co-ordinates* – Yes, that's it, it must be. Let me see now, three point one, four . . .' The Doctor began mumbling a long stream of figures, faster and faster. At last he stopped. 'Yes, that'll be it!'

Tegan never did understand quite how the 'safe' sequence worked, even when the Doctor (her Doctor) explained it to her later. All she could gather was that *if* you could observe exactly where the lightning bolts struck each time, and *if* you could then carry out some terrifyingly complex mathematical calculation at blinding speed, you *might* then be able to work out a way of crossing the second part of the board without setting off the trap.

All that concerned her at the moment was that the Doctor seemed to have got the hang of it, never mind how. He walked slowly across the board, first half then second half, and arrived safe on the other side.

'Come along, my child,' he said briskly. 'But once you pass the fifth row, be careful to tread exactly where I tell you.'

Tegan stepped cautiously on to the board. 'Don't worry. I will. I just hope you've got your sums right!'

President Borusa had left orders that he was not to be disturbed, but the Doctor could be very persuasive when he wanted to be. Convinced that the entire fate of Gallifrey depended on the Doctor being admitted to the Inner Council conference room, the bemused guard threw open the door. The Doctor stepped into the room. 'Lord President – ' He broke off, looking round in astonishment. The conference room was empty.

He turned accusingly to the equally astonished guard. 'You said the Lord President was here.'

'He is – or at least, he was, not long ago.'

'You're sure about that, are you?'

'Positive. I saw him go in – and this conference room has only one entrance. There isn't any way he could have left without me seeing him.'

Struck by a sudden thought, the Doctor went over to the transmat booth and tried the console. 'No power. He couldn't have left that way . . . Guard, go to Chancellor Flavia and inform her, discreetly, that the Lord President seems to have disappeared.'

Impelled by the sudden authority in the Doctor's tone, the guard hurried away, closing the door behind him.

The Doctor stood looking round the room. There was little to see. Just the conference table, the chairs, the wall screen, the transmat booth, and the antique harp on its stand in the corner with the portrait behind it. Shaking his head in bafflement the Doctor began a methodical search for some kind of secret door.

Sarah and the third Doctor had descended from the trapdoor into a long gloomy corridor. Dark-panelled, with occasional musty wall-hangings, the place had an atmosphere that was decidedly sinister. They went along corridors, down staircases, along more corridors, and down more staircases. Sarah found she couldn't go on. Suddenly she stopped.

The Doctor stopped too. 'What is it, Sarah Jane?'

'I'm not sure. I feel as if something was . . . pushing me back.'

'I can feel it too,' said the Doctor gently. 'It's a kind of mental attack – from the mind of Rassilon. We must be getting close to the Tomb. You must fight it, keep your mind under control'

Sarah shook her head. 'I can't. I feel as if there was something absolutely terrible waiting, just round the next corner.'

The Doctor smiled reassuringly. 'I'll just take a look, and make sure there isn't. You rest here for a moment.'

'All right. Don't be too long!'

The Doctor went round the corner, and found, as he expected, an identical corridor stretching ahead. Then, quite suddenly a tall thin-faced young man stepped out of an alcove, further down the corridor. 'Doctor!' he called urgently. 'Doctor, this way!'

The Doctor hurried forward. 'Mike? Mike Yates? How did you get here?' Mike Yates was an old friend, the Brigadier's number two for much of the Doctor's association with UNIT.

'Same way as you, I imagine,' said Mike. 'Quickly, Doctor, this way. Liz Shaw is here.'

Liz had been part of UNIT too, the Doctor's assistant when he started his exile on Earth. And there she was, waving from further down the corridor.

'Good heavens,' said the Doctor. 'Hullo, Liz. Anyone else here?'

'Come and see,' said Liz Shaw invitingly. 'You'll be delighted.'

The Doctor moved on down the corridor. 'Have you seen anything of a little chap in an old frock-coat and check trousers?'

Liz Shaw smiled. 'Him, and lots of others. There are five of you now, you know.'

'Good grief!'

'And they're all waiting for you, Doctor,' said Mike Yates.

The Doctor stopped dead. 'Hang on a minute, I must get Sarah.'

'I'll fetch her for you,' suggested Mike.

'I think I'd better go, she's scared enough already.'

Liz Shaw stepped in front of him. 'Let Mike go, Doctor. Your other selves need you, urgently.'

'No, I think *I* should go!'

Mike Yates stepped up beside Liz so that they barred his way. '*No*, Doctor.'

The Doctor stared hard at them both, thinking that his old friends were acting very strangely. Suddenly he noticed that they were looking strange too, skins white and waxen, eyes burning fanatically. Hands outstretched like claws, they stalked slowly towards him.

'No, Doctor,' screamed Liz Shaw.

'No, Doctor,' howled Mike Yates . . .

Their voices rose, distorted into unearthly screeches.

11

Rassilon's Secret

The Doctor moved determinedly forward.

'Stop him, stop him,' howled Mike Yates and Liz Shaw. Their voices blended eerily and they seemed to float towards him. The Doctor poised himself to meet their attack – then suddenly he laughed.

'Stop me? How can you stop me? You're not Liz and Mike, you're just phantoms, illusions, projections from someone's mind. You can't harm me.' He strode past – or was it through? – the two illusions, and they disappeared.

The Doctor hurried back round the corner to Sarah, where she was waiting. She looked up eagerly.

'There you are Doctor? What's happening?'

The Doctor hurried towards her, and then stopped. 'It is Sarah – isn't it?'

'Well of course it is! What's happening? Why did you leave me so long? What was that scream?'

The Doctor smiled at the stream of questions. 'Just phantoms from the past.'

'Well, I'm in the present. How about worrying about me?'

The Doctor put an arm around her shoulders. 'Yes, you're real enough Sarah Jane. Let's be on our way.'

*

'I don't like it, Doctor,' said the Brigadier. 'I feel strange. Nauseated.'

The second Doctor looked up at him. 'What you feel is fear, Brigadier. Fear projected from the mind of Rassilon.'

'Fear?' The Brigadier frowned, not sure that this was an admissible emotion for an old soldier.

The second Doctor and the Brigadier had been engaged in a very similar journey to that of the third Doctor and Sarah – except, of course, that they had been moving upwards, rather than downwards. Now that they were approaching the Tomb, at the centre of the Tower, they were feeling the same terrifying effects.

Suddenly a piercing scream rang out. 'Doctor! Doctor, help me!'

'It may be a trap,' said the Doctor. 'I'll go, you wait here.'

'I'll do nothing of the kind, Doctor!'

'Oh all right. But don't get in the way!'

They ran on together, rounding the bend and reached some more steps. At the bottom of them, one each side, were two figures flattened against the wall, apparently pinioned by some kind of light-beam. One of the prisoners was a very small girl with an attractive elfin face, the other a brawny Highlander in a kilt.

'It's Zoe,' said the Doctor. 'Zoe and Jamie!'

Both had been the third Doctor's companions on his travels for many years.

'Stay back, Doctor,' shouted Jamie.

'Why? What's happening?'

The Doctor moved nearer.

Zoe called, 'Don't come any closer! There's a forcefield, Doctor.'

The Doctor started rummaging through his pockets. 'Forcefield? I'll soon fix that! Where's my sonic screwdriver?'

'No, Doctor,' called Jamie desperately. 'If the forcefield is disturbed, it will destroy us, and you as well.'

'You've got to go back,' sobbed Zoe.

The Brigadier looked down at the Doctor. 'What are we going to do?'

The little man fished out his sonic screwdriver and brandished it. 'Get them out, of course!'

'No, please don't Doctor,' said Jamie.

'If you try to go on you'll kill all of us,' said Zoe. 'Please, go back, save yourselves.'

'I can't leave you here.'

'We could try to find another way to the Tomb,' suggested the Brigadier uneasily.

The Doctor shook his head. 'Jamie and Zoe would still be prisoners.'

'Turn back, Doctor,' urged Zoe. 'The Brigadier's right!'

'Is he? Perhaps he is,' said the little Doctor sadly, and turned away. Then he turned back. 'Is he? Wait a minute.'

The Brigadier stared at him. 'Now what?'

'A matter of memory, Brigadier.'

He moved back towards the stairway.

'A step nearer and we're both dead,' warned Jamie.

'Brigadier, stop him,' screamed Zoe.

'It's all right, Brigadier,' said the Doctor cheerfully. 'You can't kill illusions. You two aren't real. When I was exiled to Earth, you were both returned to your own people, your own times – and the Time Lords erased the memory of the time you'd spent with me. *So how do you know who we are? Answer!*'

The Doctor marched determinedly forwards – and the phantoms faded away.

'Good heavens,' said the Brigadier dazedly, and followed the Doctor up the stairs.

They hurried on their way.

The first Doctor and Tegan too were nearing the Tomb.

'Do you feel odd, Doctor?' asked Tegan suddenly.

'Full of strange fears and mysterious forebodings, you mean?'

'That's it, exactly. You feel it too?'

The old man chuckled. 'As a matter of fact, I don't! It's all illusion, my child. We're getting close to the domain of Rassilon, and his mind is reaching out to attack us. Just ignore it as I do.'

'How?'

'Tell yourself it's an illusion. All fear is largely illusion – and at my time of life, there's little left to fear!' The old man walked serenely on. 'There's nothing here to harm us, child.'

For once, the old Doctor was wrong. As they walked on down the corridor, the Master emerged from his hiding place behind a musty arras, and moved stealthily after them.

The Doctor stood in the centre of the Inner Council conference room, totally baffled. He had tapped and rapped on every possible surface. He had twiddled every ornamental moulding and projection and decoration he could lay his hands on. All to no avail.

The Doctor knew that just because he hadn't found a secret door it didn't mean that there wasn't one. A secret door could be padded so that it wouldn't give off a hollow sound when tapped. The way into a hidden chamber on Gallifrey might well be more complex than pressing the third carved moulding on the right. The Doctor scratched his head.

The guard had returned with a note from Chancellor Flavia. The Commander showed every sign of having some guilty secret, and was expected to confess his involvement in conspiracy very soon.

Meanwhile President Borusa was nowhere to be found. The Doctor considered calling in a security squad with electronic equipment. But that might cause a scandal – something he still hoped to avoid. Hands in pockets, the Doctor wandered around the little chamber, coming to a halt before the antique harp on its stand. He read the inscription. *Here is the Harp of Rassilon*. The Doctor rubbed his chin. 'Never knew he was musical – or Borusa either, come to that!' The Doctor gave the harp an idle twang – and there was a grinding of machinery, somewhere behind the wall. 'Interesting,' He twanged again. More grinding. 'A musical key,' said the Doctor. 'A particular note . . . a combination of notes . . . a tune!'

The Doctor began strumming on the harp.

Appropriately enough, the first Doctor was the first to reach the Tomb of Rassilon. He stood, with Tegan at his side, in the doorway of a tomb as big as a cathedral. A cathedral with just one occupant.

In the centre of the enormous chamber was a richly decorated bier. On it lay a motionless form, dressed in ceremonial robes. Close by there was the incongruous shape of an antiquated but complex control console, and a transmat booth. And that was all. Echoing space, silence, and the one still figure.

Tegan moved to the bier and studied the occupant. He had a face that was strong rather than handsome. He looked wise and kindly. Set into the wall by the great arched doorway there was a plinth, bearing a long inscription in some complex script. The old man spotted it immediately and began studying it. Tegan stood gazing about her in awe. Then she heard footsteps, whirled round and saw a tall white-haired man and a dark-haired young woman.

They stood in the doorway, looking wonderingly around them. The first Doctor saw them too. He stared hard at the tall man for a moment and then nodded. 'There you are at last, my dear fellow. First regeneration?'

'Second. I'm the third Doctor.'

'Yes, of course. Well, what kept you?'

The tall man drew himself up. 'Well, of all the confounded arrogance.'

'Never mind, never mind, you can tell me later. Come and take a look at this!'

A little huffily the tall man went over to look at the inscription. It caught his interest immediately. 'Fascinating,' he said and began studying it absorbedly.

Tegan smiled at the girl. 'I'm Tegan Jovanka.'

The girl smiled back. 'Sarah Jane Smith.'

It occurred to Tegan that she'd better work out some way of keeping track of the Doctors in her mind. She knew that her Doctor, *the* Doctor, was the fifth.

The old man who'd accompanied her to the Tower was the first – call him Doctor One. Now it appeared that this tall white-haired bloke was Doctor Three. In that case, what about . . .

Doctor One looked up and said suddenly. 'By the way, what's happened to the little fellow?'

Before Doctor Three could reply an indignant voice said, 'The little fellow is perfectly all right, thank you very much!' A little man in a battered old frock-coat and baggy check trousers came into the room, followed closely by an old friend, the Brigadier.

'Ah, you're here,' said Doctor Three. 'About time!'

'Of course we're here,' said the little man impatiently. 'You don't imagine anything you two can cope with would stump *me*, do you?' He spotted the inscription. 'What's all this then, eh? Let's have a look!' Pushing past his other selves, he hunched over the inscription. This, thought Tegan, just had to be Doctor Two.

The Brigadier came over to the two girls.

'Brigadier!' said Sarah, and promptly hugged him.

The Brigadier flushed, and cleared his throat. 'Nice to see you, Miss Smith . . . Miss Jovanka. Don't ask me how we got here. Like a cross between Guy Fawkes and Halloween!'

The tall white-haired man came hurrying over and shook the Brigadier hastily by the hand. 'My dear Brigadier! How very nice to see you again!'

The Brigadier said dazedly, 'Good Heavens, you as well! Nice to see you too, Doctor – though I can't exactly say it's nice to be here.'

Doctor Three glanced over his shoulder. 'Excuse me, will you, old chap? Only we've got a rather important inscription to translate, and those two will get it all wrong without me!' He hurried back to the plinth.

'Typical,' said the Brigadier. 'Absolutely typical.'

'I know,' said Sarah sympathetically. 'They haul you through space and time without so much as a by-your-leave, then leave you stuck on the sidelines just when things get interesting!'

Tegan nodded. 'My one's no better.'

'Which one's yours?' asked Sarah, and they began comparing notes.

Once they'd got things sorted out, Sarah asked, 'What's happened to the other one. The one after him,' she pointed to Doctor Three, 'and before your one?'

'The one with the hair and the scarf and the funny hat?' That would be Doctor Four, thought Tegan. 'He doesn't seem to be here. They were saying something about one of them not making it, getting trapped in the time-vortex.'

'Trust him to get himself in trouble,' said Sarah. 'Pity, I'd have liked to see him again.'

While they were talking, the three Doctors had concluded their study of the inscription. They looked at each other, clearly shaken, their faces grave. 'So that's what it's all about,' whispered Doctor Two. 'I never dreamed . . .'

'Then don't,' commanded Doctor One. 'This changes nothing. Absolutely nothing. We lower the forcefield, get the young fellow back from Gallifrey, and all go home. This doesn't concern us. It mustn't.'

Tegan caught the end of their conversation. 'What does the inscription say?'

'You really needn't trouble yourself . . .'

'I'd like to know as well,' said the Brigadier firmly.

'And me,' said Sarah. 'We've all gone through quite a lot just getting here, you know.'

The Doctors exchanged glances.

Doctor One snapped, 'Tell them!'

Doctor Two said gently, 'It's in Old High Gallifreyan, the ancient language of the Time Lords. Very few people understand it these days . . .'

'Fortunately, I do,' interjected Doctor One complacently.

'Very interesting I'm sure,' said the Brigadier. 'Never mind what it's written in, what does it say?'

Doctor Three glanced at the inscription. 'It says, Brigadier, that this is the Tomb of Rassilon – where Rassilon himself lies in eternal sleep.'

Doctor Two said, 'It also says that anyone who has got this far has passed many dangers and shown great courage and determination . . . Like me!' He pointed to the inscription, looking up at Doctor Three. 'What does that bit mean?'

Doctor Three stooped to look. 'To lose is to win – and he who wins shall lose!' He shrugged baffled.

Doctor One said quietly. 'The inscription promises that whoever takes the Ring from Rassilon's finger and puts it on shall have the reward he seeks.'

'What reward?' asked Sarah.

Gravely the old man said, 'Immortality.'

There was an astonished silence.

'Immortality,' said the Brigadier. 'Live for ever? Never die?'

The old man sniffed. 'That is what the word means, young man.'

Sarah said, 'But that's impossible!'

'Apparently not,' said Doctor Three.

'Thank you, gentlemen,' said the Master.

He was standing in the doorway with the Tissue Compression Eliminator in his hand. He moved the weapon to cover the little group of Doctors. 'I came here to help you, Doctor – Doctors! A little unwillingly, but I came. My services were scorned, my help refused. Now I shall help myself – to Immortality!'

Doctor One shook his head. 'Out of the question!'

'You're hardly a suitable candidate,' pointed out Doctor Three.

'For anything,' concluded Doctor Two.

The Master smiled. 'You think not? But then, the decision is scarcely yours. Killing you once was never enough for me, Doctor. How gratifying to do it three times over!' Stepping back, the Master raised the weapon, and took careful aim.

12

The Game of Rassilon

In his eagerness to destroy the Doctors, the Master had forgotten their companions. Or perhaps he had thought them unworthy of his consideration. It was a serious mistake.

Moving very silently for such a big man, the Brigadier crept up behind the Master. He tapped him on the shoulder. 'Nice to see you again!'

The Master spun round, snarling, weapon raised. The Brigadier delivered a right uppercut that would have dropped anyone else cold. The force of the blow sent the Master staggering back. He raised his blaster – and Doctor Three kicked it out of his hand. The Master disappeared beneath a pile of Doctors.

It had taken a very long time, but the Cybermen were ready at last. The Patrol's Lieutenant held up a remote-control device. 'The bomb is ready, Leader.'

'Excellent. Prepare for detonation.'

The Cyber Lieutenant raised his arm in signal. 'Patrol! Your orders are, move back.'

The Cybermen began to disperse.

*

Turlough watched them on the scanner, cursing the caution that had trapped him here in the TARDIS. He had no faith in the TARDIS's invulnerability. Not against a bomb of such colossal size. He looked bleakly at Susan. 'You realise what's happening?'

She nodded. 'What are we going to do?'

Turlough essayed a last, black joke. 'Die, it seems.'

The Doctor gave a final despairing twang on the harp. He had tried every tune in his repertoire, without success.

'If it's a tune, what tune can it be. A tune like . . . a tune like . . .' The Doctor gazed up at the picture for inspiration. It showed a mysterious cowled figure – Rassilon himself presumably – playing a harp exactly like the one on the stand. There was a music-stand in the picture, with a sheet of music on it. The music was painted in such detail that you could actually read it. 'A tune like the one that's been here under my nose all this time!'

His eyes on the painted music, the Doctor started to pick out the simple tune. It was a strange haunting air, an old Gallifreyan ballad now almost forgotten. As the Doctor played the final note, the hidden door beneath the picture slid quietly open.

The Doctor went down a flight of steep and narrow steps, and found himself in an underground control room – the ancient, long-forgotten Game Control.

He looked at the great Game Table with its model of the Death Zone with the central Tower. He saw the little figures dotted about, the Doctors, the companions, the Master. Only then did the Doctor turn and look at the Timescoop Control console.

Hunched over the ancient instrument there was a black-clad figure, wearing the old black cloak and head-dress of the early Time Lords. The tall figure turned and the Doctor saw with more sadness than surprise that it was Borusa, Lord President of Gallifrey. He was pulling off black gauntlets, and a jewelled coronet blazed on his forehead. His eyes seemed to burn with feverish excitement. 'Welcome, Doctor.'

The Doctor bowed his head. 'Lord President.'

'You show little surprise.' Borusa's tone was almost petulant, as if the Doctor had spoiled his fun. 'Can it be you already suspected me?'

'Not immediately. Your little charade fooled me – for a while.'

'It *was* rather neat, I thought,' said Borusa modestly. 'Pity about the Castellan – but I had to use someone as a diversion.'

The Doctor looked sadly at his old teacher. 'Oh, Borusa, what's happened to you?'

Borusa became serious, matter-of-fact, almost like his old self. 'You know how long I have ruled Gallifrey, Doctor – openly, or from behind the scenes?'

'You have done great service. It was only right that you should become President.'

'President!' said Borusa scornfully. 'How long before I must retire with my work half done! If I could only continue . . .'

'You want to be Perpetual President, throughout all your remaining regenerations?'

'Do you think my ambition so limited, Doctor? I shall be President Eternal, and rule forever!'

115

The Doctor shook his head. 'Immortality? That's impossible, even for Time Lords.'

'No! Rassilon achieved it. Timeless, perpetual bodily regeneration. True Immortality. Rassilon lives, Doctor. He cannot die. *He is Immortal!*'

The Master lay in a corner, firmly bound with ropes made from a torn-up wall-hanging.

Doctor Three was hard at work on the console that controlled the forcefield. He looked up. 'There, that's done. I've reversed the polarity of the neutron flow. The TARDIS should be free now.'

Doctor Two was standing ready at the communications area of the console. 'About time! I'll try to get through to the Capitol!'

The massive Cyberbomb stood jammed by the TARDIS door. The Cybermen were gathered at the edge of the little hollow. The Cyber Lieutenant held the remote-control detonator. 'All is prepared.'

The Cyberleader said, 'Excellent. Detonate!'

The Lieutenant depressed the plunger. The bomb exploded, sending a fountain of stones and dirt high into the air. When the smoke and dust cleared, the TARDIS was nowhere to be seen.

Inside the TARDIS, the time rotor was rising and falling.

Susan and Turlough hugged one another joyfully.

'They made it,' shouted Susan. 'They made it!'

Turlough was grinning broadly. 'So where are we going – the Tower?'

Susan nodded. 'We must be, the Doctor pre-set the co-ordinates . . .'

Pleased to have an audience at last, Borusa was pouring out all his secrets.

'Before Rassilon was bound, he left clues for the successor he knew would one day follow him. I have discovered much, Doctor. This Game Control, the Black Scrolls, the Coronet of Rassilon.' He tapped his forehead.

'But not the final secret?'

Borusa gave him a cunning look. 'The secret of Immortality is hidden in the Dark Tower, in the Tomb of Rassilon itself. There are many dangers, many traps.'

'So you transported me to the Death Zone to deal with them for you?'

Borusa was clearly proud of his ruthless scheme. 'I even provided companions to help, old enemies to fight. A Game within a Game!'

'Only you botched it rather, didn't you?' accused the Doctor. 'One of my selves is trapped in the time-vortex, endangering my very existence.'

Borusa laughed. 'Have no fear, Doctor. Your temporal stability will be maintained. I need you to serve me.'

The Doctor shook his head. 'I will not serve you, Borusa. Not now.'

Again Borusa tapped his forehead. 'You have no choice, Doctor. I wear the Coronet of Rassilon.'

'And very fetching it is too!'

Borusa ignored the taunt. 'The Coronet emphasises the power of my will. It allows me to control the mind of others. Bow down to me, Doctor.'

The Doctor resisted with every atom of his will, but the power of Borusa's amplified mind clamped down on him with irresistible strength. Slowly, very slowly, fighting every inch of the way, the Doctor sank to his knees.

A low signal chimed. Borusa adjusted controls. 'Come, Doctor.' He mounted the stairs. Helplessly, the Doctor rose and followed.

When they reached the conference room, a light was flashing on the console beside the transmat booth. A monitor screen on the console lit up, showing a quizzical face crowned by a mop of straight black hair. 'This is the Doctor – well one of them – calling the Capitol. Are you there? Are you there, Doctor?'

The Doctor found himself moving to the console. 'Yes, I'm here.'

The TARDIS materialised in the Tomb of Rassilon. Turlough and Susan rushed out – and found everyone crouched round Doctor Two, who was talking into the communications console.

'What's going on?' demanded Turlough.

No one took any notice of him.

'Can you hear me, old fellow?' Doctor Two was saying. 'We've reached the Tower, we're all safe, the barriers are down and, oh yes, the TARDIS is here. I say, we've made the most extraordinary discovery . . .'

The face of the fifth Doctor appeared on the monitor. 'I know what you have discovered. Do not transmit further. Stay where you are. Touch nothing. President Borusa is arriving to take full charge.' The screen went dead.

Doctor Two looked up. 'Touch nothing,' said the

little man indignantly. 'Touch nothing, indeed. Who does he think he is?'

Doctor One said slowly. 'Perhaps he didn't want you babbling about the Ring of Rassilon on an open channel. Even so, his manner . . .'

Doctor Three said slowly, 'You know, I think there's something wrong.'

'Oh rubbish,' said Doctor Two rudely. 'You haven't changed, I see – still finding menace in your own shadow!'

Doctor One said, 'He's right. There *is* something wrong. I feel it too.'

'We'll soon see,' said Doctor Two. 'They're here!' The transmat booth lit up, and the Doctor and Borusa stepped out. Borusa looked exultant. The Doctor's face was utterly expressionless.

Tegan ran forwards. 'Doctor, are you all right?'

'Be silent,' hissed Borusa furiously. Tegan stopped dead, as if she had run into an invisible wall.

Borusa made a sweeping gesture towards the companions. 'Be silent, all of you. Do not move or speak until I give you leave.'

The companions froze, like living statues.

Borusa turned back to the Doctors. 'Gentlemen, I owe you my thanks. You have served the purpose for which I brought you here.'

'*You* brought us here? said Doctor Three.

Doctor Two said, 'He's after the Ring of Rassilon. He wants Immortality.'

Doctor Three shook his head. 'And you were the one who didn't sense that there was anything wrong.'

Doctor Two scowled at him.

Doctor One said sternly to Borusa. 'You're a

renegade, no better than that villain over there.' He nodded towards the Master, bound and struggling in his corner.

'I'm afraid we can't allow this, you know,' said Doctor Two.

Doctor Three supported him. 'This Tomb was sealed for the best of reasons.'

Doctor One nodded vigorously. 'As soon as we're back to our own time-streams it must be sealed again – permanently.'

The Doctors ranged themselves before Borusa, barring his way to the Tomb. Doctor Two glanced at the still silent Doctor. 'Quickly, old chap, join us. Over here!'

The Doctor didn't move.

Doctor One stared hard at him. 'He can't. Some kind of mind-lock.' He raised his voice. 'Fight it, my boy, *fight it*.'

'We'll help you. Concentrate, all of you!'

Suddenly the Doctor felt the power of the linked minds of his other selves – his own mind amplified – tugging him free. With a sudden effort, he stepped away from Borusa and aligned himself with the other three Doctors.

The companions too found that they were free again. The Doctor was his old self. 'It's no good, Borusa. Together we're a match for you.'

Borusa said angrily, 'Perhaps. But you can never overcome me.'

'We don't need to. Your accomplice the Commander will have confessed by now. Soon Chancellor Flavia will be here with her guards. Can you overcome the whole High Council?'

120

'Why not? I am Lord President of Gallifrey, and you are a notorious renegade. We will see who is believed.'

A giant voice boomed, 'This is the Game of Rassilon.'

Borusa turned and took a step towards the Tomb. Instinctively the Doctor moved to stop him, but Doctor One whispered, 'Wait my boy. That's the voice of Rassilon. It's out of our hands now.'

They all turned. Rassilon had arisen from his Tomb.

Not the physical Rassilon, who slept on undisturbed, but a giant spectral presence, looming over them. The voice boomed out again. 'Who comes to disturb the long Sleep of Rassilon?'

Borusa stepped forward. 'I am Borusa, Lord President of Gallifrey.'

'Why do you come here?'

'I come to claim that which is promised.'

'You seek Immortality?'

'I do.'

'Be sure!' thundered Rassilon. 'Be very sure. Even now it is not too late to turn back.'

'I am sure,' said Borusa steadily.

'And these others?'

'They are my servants.'

The phantom's gaze turned towards them. 'Is this so?'

'It most certainly is not,' said Doctor Three indignantly.

'Don't believe him,' shouted Doctor Two.

Doctor One was silent for a moment.

Then he stepped forward and said loudly, 'Ignore

them, Lord Rassilon. President Borusa speaks the truth.'

The other Doctors looked at Doctor One in horror.

'You believe that Borusa deserves the Immortality he seeks?' demanded Rassilon.

'Indeed I do,' said Doctor One loudly.

'Then he shall have it. Lord Borusa, take the Ring.'

Borusa crossed to the Tomb and took the Ring from the sleeping Rassilon's finger.

The ghostly Rassilon spoke again. 'You still claim Immortality, Lord Borusa? You will not turn back?'

'Never!'

'Then put on the Ring.'

Borusa slipped the great jewelled Ring on to his finger.

Rassilon's voice echoed through the Tomb. 'Others have come to claim Immortality through the ages, Lord Borusa. It was given to them – as it shall be given to you!'

Suddenly the side of the Tomb, which featured three stone carvings of Time Lords, came alive, eyes darting furiously, their faces frozen and dead. A central space was empty.

In a terrible voice, Rassilon said, 'Your place is prepared, Lord President.'

Suddenly, magically, the Ring left Borusa's finger, and returned to Rassilon. Suddenly there stood Borusa, amongst the other immortal Time Lords. His body stiffened. His face became frozen and dead. Only the eyes remained alive – alive and pleading. Borusa had achieved his Immortality. An eternity of living death.

The side of the tomb darkened and Borusa and his fellow Immortals once more became stone.

'And what of you, Doctor?' asked Rassilon sardonically. 'Do you claim Immortality too?'

'No my Lord. I ask only that we all be returned to our proper places in space and time.'

'It shall be so.'

'My Lord, one of us is trapped in the vortex.'

'He too shall be freed.'

Suddenly the fourth Doctor and Lady Romana were continuing their boating trip.

The Doctor frowned, shifting his grip on the pole. Had there been something? Some odd dislocation? Imagination, he decided. 'Now then, Romana, as I was saying . . .'

The punt glided on.

Rassilon turned his attention to the Master. 'The one who is bound shall also be freed. His sins will find their punishment in due time.' The Master vanished, leaving only his bonds behind. For the moment Tegan actually thought she could see his snarl hanging in the air like the smile of the Cheshire Cat in *Alice in Wonderland*.

'Now it is time for your other selves to depart, Doctor,' said Rassilon. 'Let them make their farewells and go.' The Presence drew itself up. 'You have chosen wisely, Doctor. Farewell!'

With a crack of thunder that echoed around the Tomb, the Rassilon spectre vanished. There was left only the stillness and the silence, and the peaceful sleeping form.

The Doctor turned to Doctor One. 'You knew what would happen to Borusa!'

'I guessed,' said the old man simply. 'I suddenly realised what that proverb meant. "To lose is to win, and he who wins shall lose." Rassilon knew Immortality was a curse, not a blessing. Those who seek it are dangerous madmen, potential tyrants. This whole thing was Rassilon's trap to detect them, lure them here, and then put them out of the way.'

The Doctor looked regretfully at his other selves. 'It seems we must say goodbye. And I was just getting to know me.' He shook hands with Doctor One.

'Goodbye my boy,' said the old man. 'You did quite well. Quite well. It's reassuring to know my future is in safe hands. Come along, Susan, say goodbye.'

'Goodbye, everyone,' said Susan obediently.

Taking her by the arm, the old man led her into the TARDIS.

Doctor Two tugged at the Brigadier's sleeve. 'Time to go, Brigadier.' He shook hands warmly with the Doctor and grinned mischieviously at Doctor Three. 'Goodbye – fancy pants!' Looking very pleased with his parting shot, the little man popped inside the TARDIS.

The Brigadier came to attention and did one of his formal little bows. 'Goodbye Miss Smith, Miss Jovanka. Goodbye, Doctor – Doctors. Splendid fellows, all of you!' The Brigadier strode briskly into the TARDIS.

Doctor Three shook hands warmly with the Doctor. 'Goodbye, my dear chap. I've had the time of my lives. Haven't we, Sarah Jane?'

'Have we?' Sarah smiled wryly. 'I've only got one life, and I think it's had too much of a time!' She looked curiously at the Doctor. 'Is that. . .'

Doctor Three nodded. 'Me!' he said proudly, and bustled Sarah into the TARDIS.

The Doctor gave a sigh of relief. 'I'm not the man I was,' he said. 'Thank Goodness!'

'Why all these goodbyes?' asked Turlough. 'If we're all going home together . . .'

'Watch,' said the Doctor.

As Tegan and Turlough watched they saw one, two, then three TARDISes split off from their own TARDIS and dematerialise, leaving their original TARDIS still there.

'Temporal fission,' said the Doctor. 'Very clever chap, old Rassilon.'

The transmat booth lit up and an agitated Chancellor Flavia appeared. There were guards at her heels, phasers in hand, alert for trouble. As the little group stepped out, more guards materialised in the booth and followed them out. Chancellor Flavia was taking no chances. Glancing quickly round she hurried over to the Doctor. 'You are safe, Doctor? The Commander confessed everything. I feared Borusa might have – ' She broke off, looking about her. 'Where is President Borusa?'

'Unavailable,' said the Doctor. 'Permanently I'm afraid. It seems the old legends about Rassilon are true. He was – he is – the greatest Time Lord of all.'

'You must make a full statement to the High Council,' said Chancellor Flavia sternly.

The Doctor looked dismayed. 'Must I really?'

'It can form part of your Inaugural Address.'

The Doctor backed away in alarm. 'My what?'

Chancellor Flavia marched up to him, taking him

125

arm. It felt, thought the Doctor, rather like being arrested.

'Doctor,' she said firmly. 'You have evaded your responsibilities for far too long. The – disqualification of President Borusa leaves a gap at the very summit of our Time Lord hierarchy. We feel that there is only one who can fill this place.' She paused impressively. 'Yet again, Doctor, it is my duty and my pleasure to inform you that the Full Council has exercised its emergency powers to appoint you to the position of President – to take office immediately.'

The Doctor buried his face in his hands. 'Oh no!'

'This is a summons no Time Lord dare refuse,' warned Chancellor Flavia. She glanced meaningly at the phaser-carrying guards. 'To disobey the will of the High Council will attract the severest penalties.'

The Doctor bowed his head, apparently accepting the inevitable.

'Very well. Chancellor Flavia, you will go back to Gallifrey immediately, and summon the High Council. You have full deputy powers until I return. I shall travel in my TARDIS.'

'But Doctor,' protested Chancellor Flavia.

'You will address me by my proper title!'

Chancellor Flavia bit her lip. 'But my Lord President – '

'I *am* the President, am I not?' thundered the Doctor. 'Obey my commands at once!' He glared at the guards. 'You! Return Chancellor Flavia to her duties!'

Instinctively the guards snapped to attention – and

escorted the unwilling Chancellor Flavia back to the transmat booth.

The Doctor said, 'Quickly, you – into the TARDIS!' He bustled them inside. They heard Chancellor Flavia's anguished voice. 'Doctor – my Lord President – *wait!*' The TARDIS door closed behind them.

The Doctor dashed to the central console, and soon the time rotor began its steady rise and fall. To Tegan, it seemed he was acting with almost indecent haste. 'It'll soon be goodbye then?'

The Doctor looked up from the controls. 'Will it? Why?'

'You're going off to Gallifrey to be President, aren't you?' said Turlough sulkily. 'I suppose your Time Lord subjects will find us a TARDIS that really works and pack us both off home.'

The Doctor looked at him wide-eyed. 'Who said anything about going to Gallifrey?'

'But you told Chancellor Flavia – '

'I told Chancellor Flavia she had full deputy powers till I got back,' said the Doctor cheerfully. 'She'll be the longest-serving Deputy President in Time Lord history!'

Tegan and Turlough looked at each other, then back at the Doctor.

'You're not going back?' asked Tegan.

'Exactly.'

Turlough said dubiously. 'Won't the Time Lords be very angry?'

'Furious! said the Doctor happily.

Tegan gave him one of her disapproving looks. 'You

really mean to say, you're deliberately choosing to go on the run from your own people in a rackety old TARDIS?'

'Why not?' said the Doctor cheerfully. 'After all – that's how it all started!'